WITCHING IN A WINTER WONKYLAND

A WONKY INN CHRISTMAS SPECIAL

JEANNIE WYCHERLEY

Witching in a Winter Wonkyland:
A Wonky Inn Christmas Cozy Mystery
by

JEANNIE WYCHERLEY

Copyright © 2019 Jeannie Wycherley
Bark at the Moon Books
All rights reserved

Publishers note: This is a work of fiction. All characters, names, places and incidents are either products of the author's imagination or are used fictitiously and for effect or are used with permission. Any other resemblance to actual persons, either living or dead, is entirely coincidental.

No part of this book may be reproduced, distributed or transmitted in any form or by any means, including photocopying, recording, or other electronic or mechanical methods, or by any information storage and retrieval system without the prior written permission of the publisher, except in the case of very brief quotations embodied in critical reviews and certain other non-commercial uses permitted by copyright law.

Sign up for Jeannie's newsletter:
eepurl.com/cN3Q6L

Witching in a Winter Wonkyland was edited by Anna Bloom @ The Indie Hub

Cover design by JC Clarke of The Graphics Shed.
Formatting by Tammy

Witching in a Winter Wonkyland

*is lovingly dedicated
to the memory of my late grandfather
James Alderson Sharp
1899-1974*

*He taught us all we needed to know about the magic
of Christmas.*

I hope he would be proud

xxx

CHAPTER ONE

"*Whaaaaaaachoo!*"

I'd been skipping down the stairs but now I paused, cocking my head in disbelief at the volume of the sneeze; unsure where it had originated from.

"Gesundheit," I said when no-one appeared, and continued on my way. I really hoped none of my guests were falling ill. That would be such a shame when we were counting down to Christmas. And what a Christmas it would be. I intended to make up for last year when a fierce storm had dampened our spirits somewhat, and to that end I'd planned a week of celebrations and feasts, starting with Yule on the twenty-first and culminating in a party for the villagers on Boxing Day.

With all the baking, roasting, and general preparation well underway, I followed my nose into the kitchen, intent on discovering the source of the delightful scents that abounded throughout my wonky inn. The kitchen smelled especially fragrant. I might have known I would find Florence hard at work, baking her beloved cakes. I could have applauded when I lay eyes on the two-tier cake she was decorating.

"Ooh that looks beautifully festive, Florence!" I sang in delight.

Only a few months ago, Florence had been runner up in *The Great Witchy Cake Off*, a popular baking programme produced for Witchflix. After almost being disqualified, because she was a ghost rather than a witch, she had scraped into the final and taken the competition by storm. Now she had a book contract in the works, and a social media presence run by her capable friend—and fellow ghost—the technical wizard, Ross Baines.

The show had only recently finished airing and we were still receiving fan mail for Florence. There were days when I felt more like her personal assistant than her boss. She was 'employed' (in a manner of speaking, because I didn't actually pay her), as the housekeeper of my Whittle Inn. On days like today she spent her afternoons perfecting recipes, scribbling down her ingredients and methods, in pursuit of the perfect mix of recipes for her forthcoming baking book.

"Festive? I hope not, Miss Alf." Florence frowned. Having burned to death when her skirts caught alight as she lay a fire in the bar back in the 1880s, her dress and apron had been destined to smoulder for all eternity. The sight could be off-putting if you weren't used to it, and even now I sometimes had to waft away the stench of charred cotton myself. "It's not a Christmas cake."

I investigated more closely, creeping closer and having a quick sniff, then reaching out a finger to scoop some icing from the bowl that hovered in the air between us. Ghosts only interact with the physical world through some supreme effort of will. They make things move by utilising the power of their minds. It's a form of magick. Not much different to that which I—as a witch—employed on a daily basis.

"Miss Alf!" Florence scolded me. "I haven't finished with that yet. I don't know where your hands have been."

"They haven't been anywhere," I grumbled.

"Well that's not strictly true, is it, my dear?" Another ghost apparated into the kitchen. My great-grandmother, Alfhild Gwynfyre Daemonne, whom I'd been named after, challenged me. Gwyn, as I called her, but never to her face, had a habit of keeping tabs on everything I did. "You were upstairs playing with that owl familiar of yours a minute ago."

"Weren't you supposed to be catching up on paperwork?" Charity, my manager and at twenty-three years of age, a mere mortal fledgling, looked up from the kitchen table where she was checking through the week's menus.

"Are you lot ganging up on me?" I groused, deciding that offence was the best defence in this situation. I couldn't deny that I'd been playing with Mr Hoo, and I hadn't washed my hands, so Florence was justifiably right to be suspicious of me.

"Wha-aaa-aaa-chooooowa!"

"Who is that?" I asked, turning around at the sound of the sneeze, but nobody else seemed to know or care.

I took a moment to wash my hands at the vegetable sink while Monsieur Emietter, my French ghost chef, glowered at me. Not only did he prefer that people wash their hands in the washroom provided next door, but his absolute preference was that only ghosts prepared or went anywhere near the food. Ever since we'd had a bout of food poisoning at Whittle Inn during filming for *The Great Witchy Cake off*, he had apparently claimed that ghosts are the most hygienic way to produce meals. However, I don't speak French and have to rely on my great-grandmother's translation so there's a possibility she might have been making it up. To that end, both Charity and I were barred from touching anything in the kitchen. This was proving impossible to police because the kitchen is the warmest and cosiest place in the inn, and everyone naturally gravitates there when they have a free moment; or are hiding away from the guests and their often bizarre and eccentric demands.

I returned my attention to Florence's cake and brandished my now clean hands at her. "May I?" I asked and she nodded, albeit a little reluctantly. I scooped a small amount of the green icing out with my little finger and tasted it, blinking in surprise.

"Lime?"

"You don't like it, Miss?" Florence looked at me, her forehead creasing with worry.

Charity jabbed her finger into the bowl and had a taste too. "Oooh. Sharp! That makes your eyes water a little, doesn't it?"

"It's not unpleasant," I said, connoisseur of all things cakey. "And this is complementing which flavour sponge?"

Florence nodded confidently. "Strawberry, Miss Alf."

"Strawberry and lime?" A note of uncertainty crept into Charity's voice. "I tried that flavour as a cider once…" She pulled a face.

I pondered for a few seconds. "No I can see that working just fine." I smiled at Florence. "Can't we try the sponge as well?"

"No, Miss Alf. This is for the photographers when they come in a few days."

"Photographers?" I raised my eyebrows at Charity. I left it to my manager to deal with the reservations. But even she shrugged.

"For my book, Miss Alf," Florence scolded me. "I did mention it before. Several times."

"Oh I do remember." I tried not to sound grudging, but I think I was a little jealous of Florence's success, and rather worried that she would desert the inn and go off and live a celebrity lifestyle in London or some other big city. New York maybe.

I didn't want that to happen.

"It does look like a Christmas cake," I said. "All green and red like that." But now I could see that the pretty piped icing decorations arranged along the side of the cake, were not baubles but strawberries.

"I think you might need spectacles, Miss Alf."

Florence attended to piping delicate and tiny strawberry seeds on her decorations.

"It's all about context," I said. "We're only a week away from Christmas. You should be preparing orange and cinnamon cake, or fruit cake, or... or..." I flailed around trying to conjure up more Christmas type flavours. "Rum and coke!"

"Don't you worry, Miss Alf, it's all in hand. Now go away and stop bothering me. I have so much to do and you're not helping."

Feeling suitably chastised, I pouted. "I was hoping for a piece of cake and cup of tea for my afternoonses," I protested.

"Out. Out!" Florence shooed me away. Gwyn snorted in amusement and even Charity had to hide a grin.

"Fine. I'll starve then." I glowered at my great-grandmother.

"Chance would be a fine thing." Charity giggled. "Go back to your 'paperwork', boss. I'll fetch you up a cuppa when I'm finished with the menus."

"Thank you, Charity! That's generous of you," I said loudly as I backtracked to the door. "At least someone cares that I'm getting the proper amount of sustenance."

This time both Charity and Gwyn guffawed in

unison. Admitting defeat, I swung through the kitchen door and into the hall.

"Whaaaaachoooo!"

I paused and wrinkled my nose. One of my poor guests evidently had a touch of the winter sniffles. It seemed beholden on me, as the proud proprietor of Whittle Inn, to investigate who that might be and arrange for the proper remedies to be administered. My kitchen could provide healthy and warming soups or lemon and ginger drinks for invalids. I could even arrange for medicinal doses of brandy or whisky if required. And if those failed to make my poorly guest better, I supposed I could always consider sending for my good friend Millicent, who lived down the lane in the village of Whittlecombe. A fellow witch, Millicent's potions were second to none.

So I followed the sound of sneezing, intent on fulfilling my role as benign benefactor. Little did I know just what a cataclysm of events were about to unfold.

"Luppitt?"

"I wouldn't come any closer, my Lady. I think I may be suffering with the plague."

Luppitt Smeatharpe had sought refuge in one of the guest bedrooms on the same floor as my own suite of rooms. The exact same room where I'd originally found him, months ago, hiding out and weeping as though his heart would burst because somebody had been trying to kill him. I'd struggled to understand that at the time. Luppitt Smeatharpe, a ghost from the court of Elizabeth I, was after all, and had been for over five hundred years, dead. How, I'd puzzled, do you kill a ghost?

It had turned out that you could, but we'd put his world to rights and reunited him with his travelling minstrel friends, The Devonshire Fellows. Now he drove me crazy by constantly practising court music on his lute at all hours of the day and night.

One thing I'd found since taking over at Whittle Inn is that ghosts have few, if any, boundaries, and if you attempt to set some yourself, they are soon overstepped.

I stood in the bedroom doorway regarding Luppitt with some trepidation. I wouldn't put it past him to have contracted the plague just to spite me. Things had settled down at the inn in the run up to

Christmas and I was looking forward to the festivities. I needed a little peace and goodwill to all witchkind in my life after the year I'd had. Luppitt, more than any other ghost residing within my four walls knew that. He was also the one most prone to melodrama.

"Come, come Luppitt," I told him. "I think you're being a little OTT. Have you been sniffing the poinsettia?"

"Certai-ah-ah-ah-choooooowa!" Luppitt sneezed so hard, he propelled himself backwards by a good few inches. "Certainly not, my Lady. It's the plague I tell you." He slumped further down, head low over his stomach, his shoulders hunched around his ears.

"How, by all that's green, do ghosts get the plague?" I asked aloud, more for my own benefit than his. I knew it had to be feasible. This was Luppitt after all. Anything goes where he's concerned. "Do you have buboes?"

"Not that I know of, my Lady. Perhaps they haven't fully developed yet."

"Ever the optimist, eh Luppitt?" I clapped my hands, attempting to rally his spirits, if you'll pardon the pun. "Come on! Think positive. You know I need you—and the rest of The Devonshire Fellows—fighting fit and ready to entertain all of our guests on

Christmas Eve. The inn will be full, and everyone is already really looking forward to it."

"I'll try not to give in to it, my Lady. It may not be fatal, after all. I shall do my very best to recover." Luppitt sniffed and coughed and clamped a hand to his forehead with a groan. I pursed my lips, considering his slight figure. Given that ghosts are already fairly transparent, is it possible for them to appear paler still?

I had to admit, he didn't sound at all well. The dark circles under his eyes suggested he might be telling the truth. But I doubted he had the plague. In this day and age? Surely not.

"Maybe you should take it easy for now," I decided. "But I don't think you can stay in this room, Luppitt. It's booked out for one of our guests. You'll have to go up to the attic."

Luppitt nodded slowly, a pitiful movement if ever I'd seen one. "Very well, my Lady. It's just my head is aching so... I came in here. I merely desired a little peace."

"I feel for you," I said, because I did. It's never any fun being ill after all. "Maybe you'd benefit from a little fresh air? A walk in the woods always does me the world of good."

Luppitt shuffled off the bed, his shoulders

remaining hunched as though to ward off blows. "I'll certainly take that into consideration, my Lady. But at the moment I'm not sure I could make it that far." He bowed stiffly to me, not his usual flamboyant farewell, and disappeared from view, heading—I supposed—to the room in the attic where most of the inn's dozens of ghosts hung out.

"I hope you feel better soon," I called after him, but I couldn't be sure he'd heard me because he didn't respond again.

Back in my office I glared at the spreadsheet on my computer screen. The numbers seemed to blur into each other. "Boring." I groaned and then tapped a couple of numbers into one cell half-heartedly before rapidly deleting them.

"Oh I can't be bothered." I slumped in my chair. "It's the holidays!"

Mr Hoo, sitting on his perch in front of the cheerful fire that burned in the grate, regarded me through bright knowing eyes.

"Hooo. Hoo. Hoooo."

I tutted. "Yes, thanks. I know I have to have the

figures ready for Penelope by tomorrow... but it's Christmas!"

"Hoooo. Hoo!"

"Well it's *practically* Christmas," I griped. "You're such a wretched pedant."

He turned his head right around, like some weird extra from *The Exorcist*. "Hoo. Hoooo-oooo."

"Yes. I'd love to go for a walk." I peered with longing at the window. Outside the sky was milky white. It would be dark within an hour.

"Hooooooo?"

I glanced from my spreadsheet to Mr Hoo and back to the window. "I suppose I could always come back to this after I've finished helping with the dinner service this evening?"

"Hoo!" My little owl winked at me.

"Alright! You've convinced me!" I pushed myself away from my desk with more energy than I'd displayed all afternoon and stood up.

"Hooo-ooo. Ooh." Mr Hoo shook himself so that all his feathers puffed up.

"Yes, I'll wrap up," I replied and trotted off in search of my coat and scarf.

My owl wasn't wrong. The temperature had plummeted during the course of the afternoon and I was glad of my coat, scarf and gloves. I pulled my witch's hat down as far as I could, but it didn't come close to covering my ears. I'd have been better off investing in a pom-pom hat.

The ground felt hard beneath my feet, almost frozen. I kicked through the crispy leaves and flung my head back to watch Mr Hoo glide gracefully through the trees as he headed for Speckled Wood. I couldn't help wondering whether we were in line for a white Christmas again. Last year we'd had one, but those had been truly exceptional circumstances. Down here in Devon we were renowned for warmer air and it tended to keep the worst of the winter weather at bay.

Out in the open I could feel the resulting glow of the frigid air on my cheeks. Glad to reach the shelter of the trees, I opted to take a familiar path, the one that would lead to the centre of the wood and the clearing there where I liked to sit and mull over the events of the day.

But tonight Mr Hoo had other ideas.

When I came to a fork in the path where I would have headed right, he dropped from a branch overhead and gently buffeted his wings against me.

"This way?" I asked and he took off, leading the way down the left-hand fork. I followed, assuming we would hook around at some stage and skirt the edge of the marshes. In the heart of the forest here there was a deep pool that housed my friend Vance, an Ent. Every few days or so, I would hike out to see him and sit on the rocks surrounding the pool so I could engage in a little catching up, while he'd shower me with both love and advice and a little leaf debris.

But not this afternoon.

Where I would have expected to go right, Mr Hoo took another left turn. I frowned and faltered. Going left again would quickly take me out of Speckled Wood and into the forest at large, heading down towards Whittlecombe.

"Are you sure we want to go this way?" I called up to Mr Hoo, but he didn't stop to answer. He just kept going.

I didn't know the path that well, so I took it slowly. I didn't have my mobile on me, and a wrenched ankle or worse would not have finished the day off well. I stepped carefully and kept an eye out for rogue tree roots, while simultaneously snagging my hair or coat in low-hanging branches.

I paused to re-settle my hat safely atop my head

after it had been knocked off by a branch, and peeked up at what little sky I could see through the canopy overhead. It still had that insipid milky-white shade, but with a touch of cool-setting-sun-on-the-horizon orange tint.

"Hey?" I called to Mr Hoo. "I think we should get back. I need to—"

Mr Hoo settled on a branch seven or eight feet above my head, sending a smattering of leaves my way. I watched them fall, sunset yellow and flame red, burnished copper and—

My breath caught as I watched them settle on the ground in front of me.

Burnished copper. But not the leaves. Hair. Almost as red as my own.

A woman. Face down. One hand stretched out to her right. The other must have been tucked under her body.

A flutter of anxiety began a steady beat in my stomach just below my heart and my breath snatched noisily, a sound that hung in the still air for an interminable moment.

I thought I recognised her; the hair gave it away. One of our guests. But not a witch. Just a quiet mortal who'd seemed intent on doing her own thing, and not at all phased by the witches, ghosts and general chaos that Whittle Inn seemed to attract.

Self-contained. A loner, maybe.

A squawk in the undergrowth ahead startled me. I squeaked and glanced up straight into a pair of eyes that stared back at me through the foliage. "Who's there?" I demanded.

Whatever it was jolted backwards and scuttled away. Small enough it couldn't have been a person. Mr Hoo turned his head to watch it disappear but didn't seem concerned.

Unfortunately, the woman lying on the cold ground in front of me had not moved at all. The fluttering in my stomach morphed into a lead weight.

"Are you alright?" I shuffled forwards. The crunch of leaves beneath my feet now seemed ridiculously loud in the quiet forest. I pulled off my glove and crouched down next to her, reaching for her naked hand. I made contact and recoiled. Her hand felt stiff to the touch and her fingers were unnaturally cold.

I sank back on my haunches and took in the scene. She was dressed to go walking, in sturdy boots and an expensive outdoors all-weather jacket. Why had she forgotten to wear gloves?

It didn't really matter now. Her days of walking in the forest were over.

I rocked backwards in dismay, alarmed that—in spite of the beauty of this place—she had met her end here, alone and in the freezing cold. She'd been a guest at Whittle Inn. I should have taken better care of her.

"I'm so sorry, my lovely," I said. "I'm so very sorry."

Chapter Two

"Alf. What a surprise." DS George Gilchrist peered over the top of his notebook as I approached him the following morning. He didn't sound even vaguely astonished.

Police tape had been used to cordon off the area of the forest where I'd found the body, and it flapped noisily in the cold breeze. About twenty feet from us, a tent had been set up to protect both the remains and any vital evidence. I could no longer see the dead woman, but I knew she was there and could recall in photographic detail the position I'd discovered her lying in.

I shivered and not just from the cold.

Further away, in front of a rocky outcrop, a group of George's colleagues had gathered. We lived in an area of geographical interest, where the forest meets the Jurassic coast; trees and rocks co-existed to stunning effect. I peered at the police officers, all huddled together, but couldn't see what they were doing. Maybe sheltering from the wind.

"I found her," I told George, folding my arms and reining in the urge to glare at him. He'd asked to see me and here I was.

He and I had been an item, engaged for a short time, and although things had been a little rocky in the months since we'd split—after I'd discovered he'd been philandering with one of his co-workers—we'd gradually become friends again and our exchanges less acerbic. Only a few weeks before, he'd done me a massive favour by driving to Romania to rescue me from a rather hairy escapade, so I'd be indebted to him for a while.

"So I heard." He sighed and shook his head at me in disbelief. "If trouble comes knocking anywhere near Whittlecombe, I'll always find you at the heart of it."

"This has absolutely nothing to do with me," I protested. George raised his eyebrows. I could see the scepticism written all over his face.

He flipped a page in his notebook. "We can't find any identification on her. There's no purse or handbag. Nothing in her pockets. But PC Hetherington says you think you know who she is."

I cast a sideways glance at the tent, imagining the scene inside. "Well I can't be one hundred-per-cent sure, because I didn't turn her over. I left her in place after I checked for a pulse. But I did recognise the colour of her hair. I checked her room last night and she was a no show. So, yes, I think she was one of our guests."

"Well that's something." George sounded almost happy, and I frowned at him. It's funny what these police officers consider positive news.

"According to our register her name was Linda Anne Creary. She checked in three nights ago after making a spur of the moment booking a few days before that—"

"She's one of you lot, is she?" George gestured with his pen hand at the robes sticking out from the bottom of my winter coat.

"Are you asking whether she's a witch?" I pursed my lips.

George nodded; his face serious. "Or heaven forbid one of those hideous vampires, or a faery or something?"

Poor George. We'd only known each other

around eighteen months and in that time he'd come across more than his fair share of paranormal and supernatural beings. How he explained some of the people he'd met or the events he'd had the pleasure of working on to his superiors, I couldn't imagine. Whittle Inn and the village of Whittlecombe must surely be gaining some sort of notoriety in police circles.

Fortunately, he seemed open to it all.

Now I shook my head. "No." This had puzzled me too. "From everything I knew about her, and everything I've seen in her room, I would say no. She is not 'one of us'."

That stopped George in his tracks. "So, why stay at Whittle Inn? The Hay Loft was full was it?"

The Hay Loft was a rival inn located in the heart of the village, run by my adversary, Lyle Cavendish. Where it tended to attract holidaymakers, tourists and hikers of the more mundane kind, my wonky inn was the reserve of the strange, the gifted, the far-sighted... and the eccentric. I could only imagine that Linda fitted into that latter category.

"I have no idea. You'd need to check with them," I replied airily, and George smirked.

"It's easily done." He made a note to do so. "I'll

also need to come and look at her room and check her belongings."

"That's fine." I'd expected that to be the case.

"You said you've checked her room?" he asked. "You didn't touch anything did you?"

"I know the ropes by now," I reminded him.

"Getting quite a reputation there, Alf." George smiled. "If I didn't know you better, I'd have you pegged as a bit of a serial killer yourself."

"Oh, ha ha."

A commotion at the far end of the cordoned area diverted George's attention and he moved towards his colleagues. One of the female officers waved him over, and the group parted ways. I spotted a small fellow, between two and three feet in height, slightly balding but with longer hair at the back, and with a fairly sour complexion. He'd been handcuffed but even I, at my distant vantage point, could see the handcuffs were far too large for him.

After a few moments and a rapid exchange of conversation with the female officer, George walked back to me, kicking the leaves as he came.

"You know that man's a faery, don't you?" I nodded towards his colleagues who had closed the circle around the small creature.

George pulled a face and glanced back. "I... well—"

I couldn't believe his reticence to admit what he was seeing. "Come on, George. Don't try and tell me you all think he's a kid?"

When he didn't reply I continued, "Or a very short human?"

George's face fell. "I can hardly waltz over there to my perfectly mentally competent colleagues and tell them they're in the process of arresting a faery, can I? They'll have me on extended sick leave faster than you can turn me into a toad."

I patted the pocket in my robes where I kept my wand. "Oh I don't know. I'm pretty fast on the draw."

"Don't you dare." George's face turned slightly pale. In spite of our sombre surroundings, I almost giggled at his genuine fear but decided that would be bad form.

"Alright!" I lifted my hands to show him they were empty. "Not one of my finest moments, I'll admit." I pointed back at the group surrounding the faery. "But what's the deal with him?"

"He's under arrest. We found him here, loitering with intent."

"Intent to do what?" I asked.

He shrugged. "He was here when we arrived yesterday evening and he was held overnight in Durscombe. We brought him back out here this morning to re-interview him in situ."

"Isn't that slightly unusual?" I asked.

George pulled a wry face. "Well as you say, he's a slightly unusual character. He seems to be rather confused, or at least we're not getting much out of him that makes sense."

"So you're arresting him for murder?" This seemed a stretch.

"No, no. We have no evidence for murder."

I watched as George's colleagues began to lead the faery around the outside of the tape. They ducked under it and walked the long way around, passing us as we waited. The faery stared up at me, his face set in a sneer of derision, disgruntlement all over his face. "I wouldn't dally too long with these fools," he spat. "They'll only deprive you of your liberty too."

"I'm sorry," I told him. "I hope you're free to go very soon."

He nodded at me and trooped after the officer leading him through the forest to wherever they had parked their cars. I observed him with interest. What had he been doing hanging around a murder scene?

"Alf—" George shot me a warning look. "You can't be interfering."

"I'm not interfering," I protested. "He's a faery who was walking in the forest. Now he's been arrested but you have no evidence he's done anything wrong. That seems a little unfair to me."

"Life's unfair." George indicated the outside of the tent where a number of examiners in white plastic coveralls were conferring. "Death even more so in some cases."

I stood in the doorway while George donned a pair of plastic gloves and prepared to inspect the room where Linda Creary had been staying.

"Nobody has touched this bedroom at all?" George sought clarification.

"Florence will have made the bed and cleaned and tidied yesterday morning. She does all the guest rooms."

"I'll need to speak to her," he said, peeling back the patchwork bedspread to reveal the plain white duvet beneath.

"No problem. I'll drag her away from her duties. You'd better chat with her this morning otherwise she's liable to be incommunicado while she works on her book."

"How's that going?"

"Aaaaachooo!" The sudden sneeze from somewhere above our heads made us both jump.

"Sorry. That's Luppitt," I apologised.

"Luppitt Smeatharpe? The ghost?" George stared up at the ceiling in surprise. "He has a cold?"

"According to him it's the plague." George looked a little perturbed at this and I smiled. "Don't worry, it's not *actually* the plague."

"Whachooowa!"

I ignored the interruption. "Florence's book is going well, I believe." George turned his attention back to the bed. "She has some photographers coming in the next few days. We're going to set up all her bakes on the tables in the bar and they will take photos of them to include in the cookbook. It's going to be amazing!"

George flicked through a pair of paperbacks arranged neatly on the nightstand. "I'll have to get a signed copy from her for Stacey."

Ugh. Stacey. George's squeeze.

"Does Stacey bake?" I asked politely. I couldn't imagine her doing anything remotely practical. She and I were polar opposites in most things. For Stacey it was all about 'the look of the moment', the pristine and perfectly straight hair, fake nails and tan, exquisite make-up. As for me? Well, you know about me already.

But to be fair, my cooking prowess extends to cheese on toast and that about does it.

"There's always a first time," George replied, pulling open the drawers on the nightstand. They were empty. He frowned. "No handbag. No purse. Nothing. Did she have a suitcase?"

"A small one in the wardrobe."

George opened the wardrobe and extracted the case. It was one of those solid wheelie ones that can fit into hand luggage on most flights. Linda had left a few items of clothing hanging in the wardrobe, but that was pretty much it.

If she'd brought a handbag with her, she had taken it out with her. There was no sign of any credit cards or money. In fact, we could see very little of anything one might consider personal effects. The room seemed oddly empty and unloved. She'd been staying here but didn't seem to have genuinely inhabited the space. Not with her personality, at any rate. Linda Creary remained an enigma.

"Will your register give us an address?"

"Yes." I nodded. That would help. "I'll dig out

those details for you and give Florence a shout at the same time."

"Whachooo!"

"And maybe arrange for a Lemsip for Luppitt," George suggested. "He does not sound well."

Chapter Three

A Lemsip for Luppitt? That seemed a good idea to me.

I queued patiently at the counter of Whittle Stores, my arms full of lemons, while Rhona, the owner, served a few people in front of me.

"I hear some poor woman was found dead in the forest last night," said Mrs Crabwell, a woman I knew from Millicent's circle. She handed over the cash for three tins of baked beans, a cabbage and bottle of vodka.

"Is that right?" The woman in front of me asked as she re-knotted her plaid scarf securely around her neck. "I wondered what all the police activity was about."

"Yes." Mrs Crabwell turned to reply, "I've seen an ambulance and a succession of police cars go up."

"And the coroner's van," Plaid-scarf-woman

added. "I assumed there was something seriously amiss."

Well that's right, I thought. *That would make sense given that the coroner doesn't attend incidents with live people.*

Mrs Crabwell caught sight of me. "Good afternoon, Alfhild. I didn't see you there."

I smiled with tight lips, knowing exactly what was coming.

"On your land was it?" she asked.

I shook my head. "No, not this time." Then thinking my response had sounded a little too gleeful, I added, "A sad business though," and laced my tone with the proper amount of regret. I decided not to disclose that the woman had in fact been staying at Whittle Inn. That would just fan the flames of rumour and gossip. I'd had enough of that over the past eighteen months or so.

"I wonder who she was," Plaid-scarf-woman enquired of me, obviously suspicious that I knew more than I was letting on.

I shrugged. "I don't think they know yet." I could have kicked myself. That definitely made it sound like I had some insider knowledge. "I mean, not as far as I know. And I don't know... much." I grimaced over the women's heads at Rhona. *Help me out here*, I beseeched her with my eyes.

"Mr Bramble was in earlier." Rhona kindly sprang to my rescue. "And he reckons that they've spotted some sort of monster in the woods."

"What?" I couldn't help myself and laughed. The Whittlecombe villagers were—with a few notable exceptions—the most marvellous, kindly and lovely bunch of people you could ever hope to meet, but from time to time they did fabricate some astounding and truly ridiculous tittle-tattle.

"What sort of monster?" Plaid-scarf-woman looked a little worried.

"He was a little short on details," Rhona admitted. "Something about blazing eyes."

"Blazing eyes?" Mrs Crabwell repeated.

Rhona offered the woman her change and carefully bagged her items in a jute shopping bag. "That's what he said. It wasn't him that saw this creature, mind. He heard it from his son, Alex." She looked meaningfully at me and I tried not to curl my lip. Alex and I had been out on one disastrous date, but this being Whittlecombe, everyone assumed Alex was yet another of my failed romances.

"So Alex saw the creature?" I asked. If that was

the case I might be brazen and knock on his door so I could ask him outright.

"No, I don't think so," Rhona confirmed. "I think he heard it from someone else."

Mrs Crabwell looked disappointed, but I had to titter. This monster had apparently been witnessed by one person—just one—and yet the information, passed on from one villager to another, had become fluid and started to morph into something else. No doubt what we had here was an immersive game of Community Chinese Whispers.

I wouldn't hold much truck with any of it.

"So you didn't hear that it was the monster that killed this woman?" Mrs Crabwell asked Rhona, taking her shopping bag from the counter and testing the weight. "She wasn't ripped apart by a wild animal?"

I opened my mouth and closed it again. If I nipped that rumour firmly in the bud, I would have to admit to having been on the murder scene at some stage. I could really do without being implicated in any more suspicious deaths.

Mrs Crabwell thanked Rhona and left the shop. I watched out of the window as she crossed the road and paused to speak to Sally McNab-Martin outside the village hall. Plaid-scarf-woman paid for her groceries and then it was my turn.

"Do you think there's anything to this monster thing?" I asked, leaning across the counter as though we were a pair of conspirators.

When Rhona laughed she sounded like a young girl again, although she must have been in her late fifties or early sixties I would have thought. "I don't imagine so. You know how things get twisted."

I grunted, pleased to hear it.

"How are things up at the inn, Alf?" Rhona asked with a knowing smile and I rolled my eyes.

"Abnormal. As normal."

"But you said this lady wasn't found on your land?" Rhona rescued the lemons from my grip.

"No. I'm pleased about that at least. Unfortunately, we're talking only a matter of feet from my boundary." I pulled my coin purse from my coat pocket. "George and his colleagues are obviously out in force up there."

"At least they'll be well fed." Rhona smiled. "I'm sure Florence will see to that. You must thank her for the treacle tart she sent down for me and Stan the other day."

"She sent you a treacle tart?" I asked in surprise. "I didn't know that."

"Oh, she often sends down cakes and tarts and pies. All manner of things. She calls them her 'seconds', but believe me, they're better than anything I can produce."

I'd often wondered what Florence did with all her spare bakes. She couldn't eat them, and if Charity and I had polished off everything Florence cooked that she wasn't happy with, we'd have been the size of dustbin lorries.

"I'll certainly pass your thanks on," I agreed, picking up the paper bag containing my lemons and handing over a few pound coins.

"It was delicious. Are these for her? What's she making with these? Lemon Drizzle cake?" Rhona looked hopeful.

"Lemsip." I winked, and waved goodbye.

Outside Whittle Stores, a small crowd had gathered around Plaid-scarf-woman.

As I walked past them, I heard her regaling everyone with the tale of how a gentleman in the village had seen a devil-eyed monster in the woods.

"You know, the poor woman they found up there was torn limb from limb," she exclaimed. Several women in the crowd gasped, while their menfolk nodded as though they'd known it would happen one day.

I paused mid-step, wondering whether I should say something.

But I'd been right before, there was nothing I could say that wouldn't implicate either myself or Whittle Inn in some way, so I held my tongue and walked on.

Chapter Four

"*Yeeeeechaow!*"

I paused outside The Snug, the bag of lemons in my hands. That last sneeze hadn't sounded much like Luppitt.

"*Waa-ha-ha-chew-ah!*"

Neither had that.

"May the Goddess grant me patience," I muttered.

"Which goddess?" Gwyn asked, bustling down the corridor towards me.

"Any that could extend that particular blessing to me would be made most welcome," I told her and resumed my journey to the kitchen.

Gwyn pulled up. "You know you really need to be more specific when you're asking a deity for assistance, Alfhild."

"You mean I can't simply put a plea out there and hope the right goddess rocks up?" I called over my shoulder, making little attempt to kerb my sarcasm. "Well darn, Grandmama. I'd always assumed it worked that way. Potluck or what have you."

"Are you being saucy, my dear?"

"Certainly not!" I threw back at her, and quickly swooped into the kitchen, away from my great-grandmother's sharp ears, eyes and tongue.

"How many lemons did you buy?" Charity asked as I dumped my paper bag on one of the food counters.

"They were on offer. Four for a pound." I emptied them out and admired the sunshine yellow of the peel.

"They smell fresh." Charity joined me at the counter and picked one up to sniff it. "Mmm zesty!" She placed the lemon against her forehead. "Do you think I'd suit yellow coloured hair?"

I studied her complexion. "Why not? You suit every other colour." She'd been platinum blonde for a time now but evidently she was losing interest. "Lemon's not particularly Christmassy though, is it?"

"It is if you pop a few slices in your festive cocktails," Finbarr chipped in. I hadn't heard him come in although I probably should have done. Surrounded by his band of hyper-excited-and-permanently-hungry pixies, he was wearing his big muddy walking boots and had entered through the back door. Monsieur Emietter was gazing at my Irish witch friend with an expression that can only be described as explosive. The chef began waving his meat cleaver around, gesturing at the footprints the Irish witch had left on the floor.

Finbarr tried to placate him. "I'm on my way back out, Mon'sure," Finbarr told him. "I only came in to find Ned."

"Problem?" I asked.

Finbarr shook his head. "Not really. Only that all the comings and goings near the south side of our boundary line has meant the undergrowth and bushes in that area have taken a bit of a battering. I was hoping he'd help me fix it up, and then I can weave the perimeter force field a little more strongly in that area. I'm on my way over there now."

"Okay," I nodded. "I'll find him. Thanks Finbarr. Give me a shout if you need my help."

Finbarr clattered out of the back door, as Monsieur Emietter clucked like a Mother Hen and uttered what sounded for all the world like a string of French expletives.

"Wha-ha-ha-choooh!"

Zephaniah appeared at the kitchen door.

"Was that you?" I asked him and he looked most affronted at the idea.

"Certainly not, Miss Alf. I'm in ruddy health."

Apart from being dead, I thought. Zephaniah had died on the French battlefields during the First World War, but Gwyn had brought his ghost back to Whittle Inn where he belonged. He only had one arm, but it never seemed to hamper him in any way.

"DS Gilchrist is in the bar, ma'am. He's asking for you."

"Can't he come through here?" I asked. It wasn't like George to stand on ceremony much.

Zephaniah shook his head. "Er... he has someone with him."

"Righto." I abandoned the lemons where they were and left Charity to think about her hair colour. "Have you seen Ned?" I asked Zephaniah as I tripped through to the bar.

"In the shed, I believe."

"Finbarr's looking for him. Would you mind passing the message on? He's out on the boundary near where our guest was found."

Zephaniah saluted, and apparated away as I pushed through the glass door into the bar.

The main room bustled with activity, as I'd expect in the afternoon at this time of the year. Not only did we have an enormous cheerful blaze in the central fireplace, thanks to Florence of course, but we had a beautiful tree up in the corner, hung with pinecones and wooden ornaments and decked out with red and green ribbons. Millicent had crafted more than a dozen yule wreaths as a gift to me, and these hung from the beams and decorated the wooden surround of the bar itself. Candles had been placed on every table and bowls of nectarines and nuts were laid out for all to enjoy.

And enjoying everything they were. The hubbub here was loud enough to drown out the sound of sneezing, which was a small mercy at least. I smiled to hear the babble and the laughter, feeling proud of the inn's festive appearance, coupled with the merry vibe we had strived to create.

Our guests tended to gather here for afternoon tea because there could never be an end to Florence's offerings. We served slices of cake, decorated buns, scones with strawberry jam and clotted cream, as well as Florence's fancy cupcakes, macarons and pastries, all to people who came from far and wide to try out her wares. The tables were full of happily chattering witches and wizards, mages, sages, fortune tellers and psychics.

I spotted Gwyn, in her element, with a table of elderly witches playing bridge. I had no doubt at all that my great-grandmother and her partner would fleece the opposing pair for everything they could.

Meanwhile George loitered near the exit. It was only when I joined him there that I spotted the reason he hadn't joined me in the kitchen.

"Hi there," I said, staring down in surprise at the faery I'd seen with George's colleagues in the forest earlier.

The faery twisted his nose up at me and turned away, obviously feeling no more friendly than he had been before.

"Everything all right?" I enquired of George and he offered a wry smile, before clearing his throat.

"Yes. All fine. It's erm... just..."

I waited while the faery, who made a great show of picking at the plaster of the wall nearest him with his thumbnail, still studiously avoided my gaze. "Just?" I repeated when George faltered.

"We're looking for a safe place for Gandalf here. And I was hoping you'd be able—"

"Gandalf?" I narrowed my eyes and looked at the faery. I thought I saw the briefest smirk.

"He claims his name is Gandalf Blockhead."

"You're the blockhead if you believe that," I said, and the faery snorted at the floor.

"I don't believe his name is Gandalf. Obviously, I don't. But he's not being very forthcoming, and my resources are exhausted." George sighed. "A bit like me, really."

I nodded in sympathy as he went on, "It's Christmas. Most of my team are hoping for some time off. I have a body in the woods here and another one in a doorway in Honiton town centre. I'm supposed to be flying out to Florida in a few days for a little winter sun. My boss is having a hissy fit about our current solve rate."

I could see he was building up a head of steam and I took a quick step back. "This wee fellow has led my DC a merry dance and as much as we'd like to charge him with something—anything—we can't actually come up with anything that will stick. My Detective Super keeps telling me Gandalf here is a child and I need to contact social services and interview him in the care of a responsible adult." George was barely keeping a lid on his fury now. "That's total nonsense of course, as you and I both know."

George jabbed a thumb downwards at the faery. "I don't believe he's as innocent as he claims to be, that's for sure, and I would really like to keep an eye on him. That's why I've come to you."

I grimaced as George continued, "He claims to be of no fixed abode, so if you can put him up for a few nights and maybe get some sense from him I'd be profoundly grateful. If you can't, well we'll both be on our sweet way. Over to you."

And breathe.

I blinked at George; at his flushed face and hunched shoulders, pondering on his stress levels. "Can I interest either of you gentlemen in a quick drink?" I asked.

I had Charity show 'Gandalf' upstairs to a small room on the third floor. It had a single bed and a small en-suite, but I figured that would allow the faery all the space he needed. I took a seat at a table in the window with George and he nursed a half of Hailstone Ale while I took the opportunity to grab a mug of tea and a slice of Florence's orange and cinnamon cake.

"You seem a little... overwrought." I chose my words carefully.

George rubbed his fingers over and around his eyes. When he looked up they were red rimmed and bloodshot. "I just need a break, I think. It's been one hell of a year."

I nodded, completely understanding. Back in April he'd been kidnapped by The Mori. Then when we'd eventually found him I'd learned the horrible truth about his fling with Stacey and turned him into a toad. I'd only let him wallow in the swamp for a few days, but I guess that had been fairly traumatising.

"So you're off to Florida?" I kept my tone light and jovial.

"That was Stacey's idea," he said, not sounding particularly excited by the prospect.

I fiddled with some cake crumbs on my plate, wondering how deeply—as the nosy ex—I was allowed to probe. "Don't you want to go?"

George thought for a moment. "Yeah. Yeah. It will be nice. To get away."

"Would you rather go somewhere else?"

George smiled. "Romania was interesting. I'd quite like to go there again."

I nearly spat out my tea. "Are you serious?"

"All those old mysterious castles, and the unspoilt forest and mountains? It looked incredible. Such a shame we had to beat a hasty retreat." He grinned, impishly, his colour returning to normal. "But Stacey's not really into that kind of thing."

This was the first time I'd found myself in solidarity with Stacey. "Oh you'll love Florida," I said, as though I had expert knowledge of it.

"Yes. I expect so. It'll be nice just to get away." He took a sip of his beer. "What about you?"

I glanced around at my guests. Zephaniah had returned from seeking Ned and was now busy at the bar. Charity was serving more cake to those in need. "I won't be getting away. I'll be here."

"With Silvan?"

I shrugged. "He's away. Working." I gestured at the tree. "Christmas is not such a big deal for witches. I'll hold a proper party here on the twenty-first to celebrate Yule and the longest night. That's when we tend to gather and celebrate as the wheel turns from dark to light. We'll have a few rituals and maybe dance around the bonfire outside if the weather is dry."

"I spotted the bonfire. It looks impressive."

"Ned's been gathering wood for months." My

favourite part of Yule was lighting the fire and watching the flames.

"So you won't do Christmas this year? You did last year?" George asked, perhaps remembering the days of our fledging relationship.

"Oh, we will, but it will be all about the food and the drink, maybe a few parlour games." I was looking forward to it. I'd always been a kid at heart.

"You'll be lonely without Silvan," George said, and offered a sympathetic look. Surely he didn't feel sorry for me?

"Don't be daft." I brushed his concern away. "I'll be run ragged here. I'll have no time to get lonely, I promise."

"Besides, you'll have Gandalf to keep you company this year. Good luck with that." George had obviously relaxed now and could see the funny side of his faery situation. "Thanks for agreeing to let him stay. I appreciate it."

I tapped the table between us. "You do know I can't hold him here against his will if he doesn't want to remain here, don't you?"

"But maybe before he disappears you can find out a little more about him? He claims to have been living in the forest."

That sounded about right, but not in the way

that George and his colleagues might be imagining. They'd experience of vagrants camping out in the forest in makeshift hides or in cheap tents. However, the faery now lying on a soft mattress upstairs had—unbeknownst to most people—probably lived with the faeries in the fortress I'd visited a year ago for most of, if not his whole life.

"He'll be glad of a bed at least." George drained his half with relish. "You keep good ale here, Alf. Thank you."

"We aim to please at Whittle Inn." I rose with him and we walked to the door.

"Keep me posted about Gandalf."

"I most certainly will," I promised.

Much later I sat on my bed after my customary evening bath, rubbing moisturiser into my horrible feet and pretending I cared about them. From outside came the sound of owls hunting; Mr Hoo, having fun with a few of his friends.

I glanced towards the window. The sky was black and starless; the cloud cover low. I pondered on life and love. Did Mr Hoo have a special someone? If he did, he didn't live with her; he lived with me. But then I—supposedly—had Silvan, and he didn't live with me either.

"Hmmm," I said, out loud. I caught the wistfulness in the sound and gave myself a mental shake. This was early days for Silvan and me, and we lived very different lives. Honestly I wasn't entirely sure what he did to make his money, except he'd always told me he worked for the ones who would pay him the most. What these people paid *for* I had never probed too deeply, worried what I would find out perhaps. He was a mercenary. A dark witch. An expert in the defensive arts. He was a warrior among witches. When we'd first met—I'd hired him to train me to become more of a warrior myself so that I had what I needed to beat The Mori—I'd assumed he had neither scruples nor morals, but now I found myself absolutely convinced of his integrity and compassion.

He was a smart Aleck and a wisecracking jester, but he'd stolen my heart. Sometimes, when I lay alone in bed at night and closed my eyes, I could sense him near me, almost as though his spirit could travel the miles to find mine. Tonight, I missed him more than usual, I suppose because George had drawn attention to the fact that the festive season was upon us and I would be alone.

"I'm luckier than some," I told myself. "I have Grandmama and my ghosts, and Charity is working all through Christmas and New Year too. We'll have a riot."

My mobile phone, turned face down on the bedside table, started to ring. I quickly rubbed my hands dry on my towel and grabbed the phone. The display told me an unknown number was calling.

I thumbed the screen. "Hello?"

"Hey, Alfie?" a familiar voice said.

I gasped in surprise, but I suppose I might have known. "Silvan?"

"Who else?" He chuckled. I smiled to hear it.

"I've been sitting here thinking about you."

"Aww have you?" His voice sounded distorted. It wasn't a great line. He could have been calling from the bottom of the ocean. "That's nice. You must be missing me." He laughed again.

"Maybe," I replied. It wouldn't do to give him a big head. "George was here this afternoon and we were talking about Yule and Christmas."

"Oh right. He's okay, is he?"

"I found one of my guests dead in the woods last night?"

"I heard about that. That's why I decided to call you." *He'd heard about it? How?* It amazed me sometimes how quickly word flew around the witching community. Presumably Gwyn or Millicent had spoken to Wizard Shadowmender, or Penelope Quigwell, and they had passed word out to witches elsewhere. "I wanted to make sure there was no threat to you or the inn?"

My insides melted. He'd been worried. "Not as far as I know," I reassured him. "She was staying here but I found her outside the inn's boundaries. There's nothing to suggest—"

"Whachooowa!"

The sneeze exploded loudly in the air around me.

"What was that?" Silvan asked.

I glared up at the ceiling. It had sounded as though it originated just above my head. "Luppitt has a cold."

"Whacheeee! Whacheee! Whacheee!" A fast series of high-pitched sneezes.

"Ghosts get colds?" Silvan sounded perplexed. "I never knew that."

I rolled my eyes. "Neither did I. He's making a right song and dance about it."

"I guess that's the travelling minstrel in him."

"Ha!" I grinned down the phone. Hearing his voice reminded me afresh just how much I missed him. I hesitated. "Silvan?" I didn't want to sound like a wheedling needy girlfriend.

"Still here," he said when I didn't continue.

How should I approach this? "Where are you at the moment?"

His turn to hesitate. "You know I can't tell you that. If I told you—"

"You'd have to kill me, I know."

"Good goddess, no. I wouldn't kill you, though I might be tempted to at times. The problem is that someone else might. It's best you don't know what I'm doing when I'm away. You know that."

I sighed. I did know that.

"I was hoping you'd make it home, or here to the inn, for Yule, that's all." Ugh. That did make me sound wretchedly wet. I waited for him to mock me, but he didn't.

"I know." His voice was soft. "I'd be there if I could."

"I know you would," I said, and tears pricked at my eyes.

"WhaCHEW!"

"Alfie, it sounds like Luppitt needs some TLC there. I'm going to have to go anyway. I love you."

"I love you too." I told him, but he'd already gone, and I was speaking to dead air.

Outside the owls were quiet now. It wasn't quite ten yet so maybe they'd had their fill of field mice or bats or whatever it was they were gorging on tonight. I grabbed my dressing gown and made my way down to the kitchen.

"What are you up to, Alfhild?" My great-grandmother's querulous tones drifted my way as I leaned against the counter waiting for the kettle to boil. I'd sliced up a lemon and added a shot of whisky to a mug.

"I'm making a mug of my finest cold remedy for Luppitt," I replied as Gwyn's form apparated next to me, a little delayed in comparison to her voice.

Gwyn glanced down, scrutinizing the contents of the mug. "How's he going to consume that, my dear?"

"What do you mean?"

"He's dead, Alfhild. He can't swallow any drink that you make him."

I blinked at my great-grandmother in realisation. Of course. Luppitt as a ghost couldn't interact physically with a mug of liquid. "Oh batpoop," I moaned.

"Quite."

"I'd forgotten." The kettle whistled its readiness

and I poured some hot water into the mug anyway, giving it a hard stir. "Don't worry," I said when Gwyn arched an eyebrow at me. "Waste not, want not. I'll have it." I took a sip. The water, cooled slightly by the whisky, was still too hot.

The sound of sneezing drifted down the stairs and into the kitchen. I replaced the mug on the counter. "Maybe it will ward off his germs."

"You're worried about catching Luppitt's flu?" Gwyn asked.

Oh it was flu now, was it? The diagnosis had escalated a level. "He thinks it's the plague," I reminded her.

"It's influenza. And if you'd lived through the epidemic of 1918-1919 as I did, you'd know how deadly it can be." I nodded. She'd told me of the millions who had died worldwide, mainly young adults between the ages of twenty and forty. A few of her own friends had perished. How sad that so soon after that horrendous global conflict which had killed so many, that the rest of a generation had been wiped out.

"He needs tucking up in bed, poor thing." I tried sipping my drink again. The whisky and lemon concoction worked for me as a nightcap.

"They all do."

I blew the steam away from the surface of the liquid. "What do you mean?"

"I mean it isn't just Luppitt who has influenza. The rest of the Devonshire Fellows appear to have caught it too."

Chapter Five

"Millicent? I really need your help again."

Millicent Ballicott, my nearest witchy neighbour lived in pretty little Hedge Cottage down Whittle Lane. A lady of indeterminate age, she was a woman of eccentric tastes. Especially when it came to her clothing.

Today, as I stood shivering on her front step, I could only compare my friend to a seaside deckchair. I'd caught her wearing a pair of striped white and mint trousers, and a forest green jumper, along with bright red slipper-socks. "Almost matching today, Mills," I murmured as she stood back and I squeezed past her to enter her living room.

"I heard that," she retorted and closed the front door after me. "I knitted this jumper myself, you know?"

I bit back the temptation to tell her it looked as

though she'd dropped a few stitches, and simply smiled my appreciation instead. "Very nice. Really."

After extracting myself from the ecstatic welcome Jasper the lurcher and Sunny the Yorkshire Terrier treated me to, I plonked myself down on Millicent's comfortable sofa. "Oh is *so* nice to take the weight off my feet," I said.

I'd had a rather full on day so far. The inn was packed to the rafters and, thanks to the cold and frosty morning, everyone had demanded a cooked breakfast. Somehow Finbarr's pixies had escaped him, snuck into the kitchen and run off with all the grilled bacon. Monsieur Emietter had—according to Gwyn—threatened to slaughter all the accursed creatures while they slept and serve them up in a pie on Boxing Day. Meanwhile Florence was in a complete tizz about her visit from the photographers, which had left poor Charity to grill more bacon because I had to manage the waiting aspects of breakfast with just Zephaniah helping out with beverages.

I peered up at Millicent hopefully. "Is it tea you're after?" she asked me, and I grinned.

"Yes please. It's been one of those days." I reconsidered. "One of those weeks actually."

"I heard it was you that found the woman in the

woods the other day," Millicent called from her tiny kitchen.

I swivelled in my seat so I could address her directly. "Yes. Very sad."

"Do they know who she is yet?" Millicent's voice sounded muffled and I could see her large stripy rump pointing out at me as she buried her head in the cupboard where she kept her biscuits.

Yippee! Biscuits!

But oh, those trousers.

"She was staying at my inn, so we have her registration details, but that's about all."

"How did she die? Do you know?" Millicent returned to the living room with a tray containing mugs, milk and a plate of biscuits. "I'm just waiting for the kettle."

I helped myself to a chocolate Bourbon. "I don't know. I asked George yesterday but they're waiting for the post-mortem results." I munched for a moment, lost in thought. "It didn't appear messy. I was pleased about that."

"I'm sure you were." Millicent disappeared into her little kitchen once more and a few minutes later came out with her teapot shrouded in another of her knits. This time it was a knitted tea cosy covered with gaudy flowers and miniature button bees and butterflies. "I'm sure George will get to the bottom of it."

I nodded and reached for another biscuit.

"Are you hungry, Alf?" Millicent asked as she took a seat opposite me and placed the tray on her coffee table. "You could at least wait for the pot to brew."

"You know what they say, 'feed a cold and starve a fever'."

"Do you have another cold? I have some more of my blackberry cordial potion under the sink if you want it." She shifted in her seat as though to stand up again and, shuddering at the memory of her blackberry cordial, I held my arm out to stop her.

"No! No, I'm fine thanks. It's not me. I'm just trying to keep the germs at bay. It's Luppitt. Well actually it's all of The Devonshire Fellows. They've caught the flu."

"All of them? Well that surprises me. I didn't know that ghosts could catch the flu." Millicent picked up the teapot and poured a little liquid into one of the mugs through a tea-strainer. Like Florence her preference was for loose leaf tea, whereas I was throw-a-teabag-in-a-mug-kind-of-girl. "Just another minute on that, I think," she said.

"That's what everyone has been saying," I told

her. "And I didn't know either. But believe me, they're suffering. Living at Whittle Inn with my crew has certainly taught me a thing or two about ghosts. It's been a steep learning curve." I waited patiently for my tea and when Millicent handed me my mug full of amber liquid, I nabbed another biscuit. Purely for the dunking opportunity it presented.

I settled back on the sofa in contentment, Jasper snuggling next to me, Sunny sniffing the rug in front of me, on the scrounge for any biscuit crumbs that might have dropped her way.

Millicent, sitting across from me in her comfortable armchair, raised her eyebrows. "So you said you needed my help? Or are you just here to eat me out of biscuits?"

I eyed the half-dozen still available on the plate. "But I haven't eaten them all yet."

"Help yourself."

"Ta much." I grabbed another two and settled one on my lap while I dunked the first one. You have to get the timing just right when you're dunking biscuits. Experience is everything. You can't immerse a chocolate Bourbon for too long as it will just disintegrate, and no-one wants that mess at the bottom of their mug. I concentrated.

Dunk. One and two and ready to eat. Perfection.

"Mmm." I turned my attention to Millicent. "Yes. I was hoping you could help me out with the ghosts who have the flu. Honestly. All that coughing and sneezing and spluttering? It sounds like some kind of Victorian consumption ward at the inn at the moment. The guests are beginning to notice."

Millicent looked nonplussed. "Well what do you expect me to do? I can't give them my blackberry cordial."

I frowned. I'd anticipated this hurdle, of course. This was the same issue I'd had with my lemon remedy for Luppitt. The ghosts couldn't physically drink Millicent's remedies either. "I had hoped you'd know the solution. Isn't there anything you can do?" I asked.

Millicent shook her head. "I only work with mortals, Alf. Ghosts aren't my thing, they're yours."

"So..." The final Bourbon lay forgotten in my lap. "There's nothing that can be done *at all*? I just have to let the flu run its course and hope no-one else gets it?"

"Can you keep the infected ghosts segregated somewhere? Stop it spreading any further?"

"In the attic, I suppose." I pondered on this. That would mean turfing my more cautious and people-shy ghosts out of their habitual hiding place up in the rafters and allowing them the run of the rest of the inn. Many of them preferred being tucked out of sight. Most of my guests were witches and wouldn't mind the ghosts, but there were always the odd one or two mortals who might find it all rather unnerving. I'd just have to forewarn them.

Millicent stared absently at the wall behind me for a minute before coming back to the present. "There is one other possibility," she said, hesitating slightly.

"Go on?"

She leaned forward in her chair. "Once. A long time ago. I heard about a ghost doctor."

"A ghost doctor?" Memories of Perdita Pugh, the ghost whisperer, sprang to mind. I grimaced inwardly. Thank heavens I'd never have to have anything more to do with her or her strange dog, Chi. "One that tends ghosts?"

"Yes. A ghost doctor, as you'd imagine, helps sick ghosts... and *is* a ghost."

"That sounds just the ticket. Where can I find one?"

Millicent snickered softly. "No idea, Alf. You'll have to do the donkey work on that, I'm afraid."

I slumped. How disappointing. I'd been hoping Millicent would have all the answers.

"You could always ask that weird ghost whisperer person you had at the inn, year before last."

Perdita. Urgh. Just what I'd been trying to avoid doing. I groaned and tried not to sound too glum at the prospect of talking to her again. "Yes, she would know, wouldn't she? I'll have to get in touch."

"I would." Millicent's gleeful smile told me she remembered exactly what I'd thought of Perdita Pugh.

Beside me Jasper had turned away and was munching hard and rapidly on something. I leaned over to find out what it was and realised he'd grabbed my biscuit. "Why you little—"

"Dear?" Millicent asked, smiling at her hound. "He is, isn't he?"

I departed Millicent's cottage feeling a little bloated. That would be the half packet of biscuits I'd polished off. Oh well, I ruminated, I wouldn't require much sustenance at dinnertime. For now, I needed to get back to the inn and help Charity prepare for the evening service. The shadows were growing longer, and twilight wasn't far off. First things first though, I still needed to buy some stamps and post a few letters. I turned right and headed down into the village proper to complete my errands

It didn't take long, and a few minutes later as I exited the Post Office and attached the stamps to my envelopes, a sudden commotion distracted me.

"Help! Help!"

I swivelled around. A woman in her forties, dressed for walking, her blonde hair streaming loose behind her, rushed towards Whittle Stores.

"Are you alright?" A gentleman held his hand out to slow her pace. She stopped in front of him and doubled over, breathing in deep, ragged gasps. A few other customers came out of the shop and enquired as to her wellbeing. I walked slowly towards them, loathe to become involved in any drama, but unable to stop myself from being a little nosy.

The woman straightened up, panting, her eyes wild with fear. "I was walking in the woods," she puffed. "Beyond Whittle Folly." She looked about at the crowd gathering around her then lifted shaking hands to her face. "I saw it. I saw the monster. The one with the glowing red eyes!"

CHAPTER SIX

"Do you believe there's a monster in the woods with glowing red eyes?"

After I'd finished serving our guests dinner, I'd left Charity and Florence to clear up and had climbed back upstairs to my study to make a couple of phone calls. Firstly I rang Mr Kephisto, a wizard friend and proprietor of *The Story Keeper*, a bookshop in nearby Abbotts Cromleigh. I'd often had to rely on him in the past. He was an archivist for everything witch or wizard related. I'd visited his attic where the records, books, pamphlets, letters, postcards, tapes and digital recordings, prints, paintings and etchings were stored several times. He knew something about everything, but if he didn't know he made it his mission to find out. He was also the architect of the forcefield that ran all the way around the boundaries of Whittle Inn and kept my grounds secure.

For the most part, anyway.

"Anything is feasible," Mr Kephisto responded, and I heard a note of hungry intrigue in his voice. I could imagine him diving into his collection in search of relevant information. "But I've never read any tales of wild demons or savage creatures in that part of Whittle Forest."

"What could it be?" I wondered out loud.

"The woman said this thing she saw was fairly large?"

"Yes." As the crowd had grown around her, she'd become increasingly hysterical, but I'd managed to ascertain that the creature was about the size of a small horse.

"Oh, that's a shame. I was hoping it might be a chupacabra." Mr Kephisto sounded a little disappointed.

"A chupa—? What?"

"Chupacabra. It's a relatively new discovery; mainly found in South America I believe. But you never know. Someone might have relocated one to a private zoo, and it could have managed to get loose."

"But what is it?" I doodled the word onto the page in front of me. Mr Kephisto had given me

Perdita Pugh's number and I intended to call her next. Talking to the old wizard about the creature in the woods made for wonderful procrastination.

"It's a relatively small animal. About the size of a dog. People who've seen it speak of its red glowing eyes and its glistening fangs. It lives in the forest and preys on goats and cattle. It kills animals by sucking their blood, like a vampire."

"Really? That's hideous," I grumbled. "I hate vampires."

"Well I wouldn't worry. It sounds like your creature is too big for that," Mr Kephisto cheerfully reassured me. Wizards are funny beings.

Mr Kephisto um'd and ah'd for a minute. "It's probably too small to be a minotaur. It could possibly be a werewolf."

"But I've had werewolves stay at the inn before now. Why would one of those be roaming the forest? They could have a perfectly pleasant bedroom here with me."

"I hate to break it to you," Mr Kephisto told me in hushed tones, "But there's more than one inn in Whittlecombe. Maybe he's staying at The Hay Loft." Mr Kephisto sounded surprised that I hadn't thought of that.

I pouted. "I can't see that myself." Lyle Cavendish wouldn't have allowed it.

"Alright. Perhaps he just likes living in the wild?" Mr Kephisto tried.

"In December? The ground is frozen hard. It's below freezing at night, and for part of the day too come to think of it." Besides, it would be a stretch to call the forest around Whittlecombe wild.

"It's an odd one," the old wizard admitted. "I'll look into it. Keep me posted if you hear anything new, Alf?"

"Will do," I said, preparing to hang up.

"Oh and pass my best wishes on to Perdita."

Perdita.

It took her a while to remember who I was, but when she realised, she was as effluent as ever.

"Oh my word, Alf," she cooed in her new-age hippie drawl. "It's so good to hear from you. How are you? Have you still got all that wonderful hair?"

"Yes—"

"And did you have any joy losing weight at all. You know you'd look amazing if you shifted a few pounds. Not that I'd ever judge anyone for their size, you know what I mean? But it's so much easier on your joints if you can maintain a decent body ratio. Especially now you're getting a bit older."

"Thanks, yes—"

"Sorry. I'm probably being a bit forward. But I've found since I changed to a vegan-macro-panko-seed and root diet, the pounds have simply dropped off me."

"Oh maybe I should try—"

"I thought little Chi might benefit as well but it made her very ill. How's your owl, Alf?"

"He's fine, thanks."

"Oh that's good. Such a cute little fellow. And very wise. But that owls all over isn't it?"

"Yes. I think—"

"And what did you decide to do about your ghosts, Alf? You were thinking of a few exorcisms and banishings if I recall, because there were large numbers of ghosts at the inn, weren't there? It all seemed a little chaotic and free form when I was there."

She paused for breath. I jumped in before she could start again. "Oh there's even more here now," I chipped in, keeping my tone frothy. I didn't want to encourage her to start thinking about getting rid of any of my spirits again. "I don't turn any of them away. I've made that our policy. All ghosts are welcome at the inn."

"Oh that's so sweet. You're such a good person, Alf."

"I don't know about that—"

"No, no. You really are. And a wonderful ghost whisperer in your own right."

I was touched. "That's very kind of you to say so, Perdita." She could be a darling when she wanted to be. "But you're the bees' knees and I'm only walking in your footsteps. I actually called to pick your considerable brains."

"You need my help? I'm honoured. I'm happy to help any way I can."

I breathed a little easier. "Smashing. Mr Kephisto—"

"Oh how is he? I haven't spoken to him in absolute eons!"

I tapped my pen against the paper I'd been doodling over, admiring a complex pattern of leaves with a pair of eyes peeping out from among them. Talking to Perdita was like herding goldfish. "He's really well, thank you. I've literally just got off the phone with him because I needed your most up-to-date number." I didn't want to admit that I'd misplaced her details or thrown them away or something. I hadn't imagined I'd ever need her help again.

"Bless him. Such a cute chap."

Cute? I pulled a face. Mr Kephisto had always been pretty cagey about his actual age, but he looked like a man well into his seventies. I had a suspicion that he was probably far older. "Isn't he?"

I slammed my pen down. I had to get to the crux of the matter or Perdita would keep me chatting forever. "And so wise." I changed tack. "In fact, he confirmed what I thought... That you were definitely the best person to help with a little problem I have here at Whittle Inn."

"Oh, Alf! It's so wonderful of you to invite me down—"

What? Invite her down? No. That was the last thing I wanted. Perdita's presence here at the inn over Yule would be insufferable. "Erm—"

"Unfortunately I've been invited up to Scotland to investigate a troublesome spirit at Glamis Castle. I'm in the process of packing up now."

I exhaled in relief. "Oh that's such a shame!"

"I know it is. Maybe I can fit you in during February?"

"There's absolutely no need to do that, Perdita. You can probably act as my adviser over the phone which will save you a huge amount of bother. I would hate to inconvenience you in any way."

There was a silence over the airwaves, and I wondered whether Perdita was offended by the suggestion that I didn't require her physical presence. "If you don't mind," I added, hastily making amends. "I mean... I appreciate how much demand you're in... so a telephone consultation would be invaluable to me. I really can't think of anyone whose intelligence and input I value more." When she was still silent, I continued, "And... and we can catch up next Spring, when the weather is better, and you have time in your hectic schedule to visit us all."

I could imagine the cogs of her mind whirring as she processed all I'd said. "Why yes, I can see that any assistance I can offer, no matter how small, would be beneficial to you, Alfhild. Right here and now. I'm happy to help as much as I can, of course. What do you need to know?"

"Are you having a nap, Alfhild?"

I lifted my head from my desk where I had placed it in despair after I had finished my conversation with Perdita. The coughing and sneezing echoing around the inn appeared to have increased over the course of my two telephone conversations. Could it be that every ghost within a ten-mile radius had fallen ill?

"No. I—" I blinked at Gwyn in surprise. What was she wearing?

"Don't stare, my dear. It's rude."

"I just needed a rest, Grandmama." I gawked at her, not quite comprehending her strange attire. As ghosts go, Gwyn possessed a varied wardrobe although I had no knowledge of how or where she stored her ghostly apparel. Now she stood before me wearing clothes I'd never seen before. A pale cream dress, a long pinafore apron and some strange headgear. "Why are you wearing fancy dress?"

"What are you blathering about? This is my nurse's outfit. I'm proud that I can still fit into it."

"You were a nurse?" She'd never told me that before.

Gwyn nodded. "During The Great War."

I rocked back on my chair, shaking my head. "You're full of surprises, Grandmama."

"We all had to do our bit for the war effort."

"Did you go to the Front?" I'd read up on the history of some of the great battles in France and Belgium after Zephaniah had told me his story. The conditions at the medical stations had been incredibly unpleasant.

"I served eight months in Flanders in 1917. I was glad to come home," Gwyn replied, her voice giving nothing away. "But for most of the war I remained here in Devon, receiving troops when they were transferred to several of the war hospitals set up in Exeter."

I exhaled nosily. "Well, I never knew that!" But that didn't alter the fact that she'd chosen this particular get-up to wear this evening. "But why…?" I wiggled my fingers at her dress.

"We currently have nine ghosts down with influenza, Alfhild. They require nursing."

"Nine?" Now the level of sneezing made sense. "And you're the one to do it?"

"In the absence of anybody else, it would appear so," she replied, arching an eyebrow. "At least I'm taking their afflictions seriously, Alfhild."

"Do you mind?" I replied, a little cross at her insinuation. "I am doing my level best to track down a doctor who can help. I haven't been having much luck so far."

"Couldn't you find one the same way you found Ross Baines?" Gwyn asked.

I'd considered that. I'd needed a computing

whizz and I'd gone to the financial district in London looking for someone to help. In the end, finding Ross Baines had been a bit of a fluke. There was a chance I could employ the same tactic, but how many doctors die with their boots on? Imagine the sheer number of people who have passed from this life while in hospital. The numbers were scary. I couldn't simply hang out in a geriatric ward and hope I stumbled across the ghost light of a specialist for infectious diseases. No. That would be entirely too chaotic.

I smiled at my great-grandmother. "Don't worry, I have a lead." *Of sorts.* "Thanks to Perdita Pugh."

Gwyn sniffed. "I didn't like that woman very much."

"I think you made that perfectly plain, Grandmama."

"I hope you're not suggesting I was rude, Alfhild." Gwyn smoothed out her apron and changed the subject. "While you're searching for Perdita's doctor, let me tell you how I'm going to proceed. As you suggested I'm going to ban all the ghosts who are currently healthy from the main attic. You'll have to find space for them elsewhere and hope they stay out of mischief. Then I'm going to set up the ward—"

"Set it up?" I asked.

"I'm having the attic scrubbed from top to bottom and then we'll set up some beds. The goddess knows we have more bedframes and mattress than one inn decently needs."

"But—"

"I know what you're going to say, my dear. Ghosts don't need physical beds. And that's true of course. But I would like to give them the semblance of normality."

"But—"

"And cosiness. Particularly at this time of year."

"That's great, Grandmama. It's just—"

"Many of our poor ghosts would have celebrated Christmas rather than Yule, you know? None of them are actually witches."

I nodded. "I do know. I'm just thinking that cleaning out that attic will take weeks." The contents of the massive attic had been thinned out a little during the eighteen months I'd owned the inn, but enough stuff still remained up there—some of it centuries old—to fill several dozen antique shops.

Gwyn considered this. "I'll make use of the Wonky Inn Clean Up Crew as you insist on calling them. Don't worry, Alfhild. Even if I only use a fraction of the space, it will still make a difference."

I regarded my great-grandmother with fondness. She made me smile. So stubborn and yet so dynamic.

"Go for it, Grandmama. I'll carry on trying to track down the doctor Perdita recommended. You start making our Devonshire Fellows well again.

CHAPTER SEVEN

"Hi. It's Alf. I wondered how you were doing?"

I'd lightly tapped on Gandalf's door, unsure whether he would be sleeping or not.

"What is it?" a curt little voice asked.

I waited patiently; my ear close to the crack of the door. I thought I heard the faery shuffling inside. Eventually I said, "If you don't want to be disturbed that's fine with me. I just wanted to check you are comfortable and have everything you need."

A few seconds later the door opened a crack, and the small fellow's sharp features peered up at me. His eyes were the palest of blues, like a watercolour sky.

"All that coughing and sneezing is getting on my nerves," he griped.

"I do apologise. I agree it sounds like we're running a convalescent home for sufferers of bronchitis and pneumonia. We are trying to remedy the situation as quickly as we can." I rapidly ran through the rooms we had available, but nothing suitable sprang to mind.

"Also that stench of boiled vegetables?"

"Yes?" I asked, pretty sure that the inn did not stink of boiled vegetables. Monsieur Emietter had created a sumptuous beef casserole this evening, and a vegan equivalent, both served with turnip and carrot mash; they'd been exquisite.

"It's making me nauseous."

"Hmmm," I responded, trying not to smile. It seemed to me that the faery was intent on being as difficult as possible. I wondered if he was peckish.

"I'm sorry to hear that. What would you prefer?" I asked. "My kitchen can prepare anything you desire."

"I'm not hungry," he said, his tone indifferent.

I took a moment and then nodded. "Well as I said, if you do need anything just give me or one of my staff members a shout." I nodded and retreated along the corridor.

"I like sweet things," he called after me. I halted and turned my head to smile back at him.

"You do? Terrific! So do I."

I carried a tray of sweet treats and a teapot upstairs, with a cup for Gandalf and a mug for myself. We sat cross-legged on the floor and I watched while the faery stuffed his face full of cake and pastries.

"What's this one?" he asked; his cheeks as full as a hamster. "It tastes like an elf's garden."

I used my fork to break a chunk away and chewed thoughtfully, pondering on what an elf's garden might taste like. Finally, after I'd swallowed, I giggled. "You're right. I'm going to hazard a guess that this one is elderflower and marjoram."

"Eww." The faery pulled a face, but I noticed he didn't spit anything out.

"What about this?" He tried the next slice.

I took another forkful. This seemed more seasonal. "That's easy. Orange and cinnamon. With a dark chocolate frosting."

"Hmpf."

"Don't you like this one?" I asked. "It's one of my favourites."

"It's so-so."

I took a chunk of a pastry. "This is Florence's version of an egg custard. There's lots of vanilla in this one. Yummy."

The faery tried a bit, pulled a face of absolute disgust... and promptly stuffed the rest into his mouth. He had an appetite that would have given Finbarr a run for his money.

"Who's Florence?" He paused for a rest.

"Florence is the housekeeper here at the inn. She's a ghost."

"Is she the scorched one?"

"Yes." He'd seen her then.

"Poor girl." He belched softly. "And the one with one arm? He's a ghost too?"

"Zephaniah? Yes."

Gandalf nodded; his face serious. "You attract some queer creatures here."

I hid a wry smile. He could say that again.

"They all have such silly names too."

Now he sounded like George. I laughed. "None so silly as Gandalf Blockhead."

Now it was his turn to laugh. It was the first time I'd seen him smile. He didn't look remotely severe when he forgot to be stern and grumpy. "Those police officers would believe the moon was made of green cheese, they're that gullible."

"You gave them a hard time."

"They deserved it."

I let that slide and he drained his cup of tea and reached for more cake.

"So what is your real name?" I asked, keeping my voice smooth and calm as though I wasn't particularly interested. I didn't fool him for a second.

He glared at me, full of suspicion once more. "Who wants to know?"

"Well, me, I suppose," I confessed. I carried on, pretending to be unconcerned, and poured more tea for him.

We sat in silence for a time. He chewed and swallowed, regarding me all the while. I began to feel a little self-conscious under his scrutiny and scratched at my nose. "You're the one, aren't you?" he asked eventually.

"The one?"

"The one that intervened in the stand-off between the faeries and Mara the Stormbringer."

"Ah." He knew about that, did he? "Yes." It seemed easiest to tell the truth. I waited for an explosion of disapproval that didn't come.

"I knew Harys." Harys was the changeling given to Mara after a little negotiation between myself, the faeries and Wizard Shadowmender the previous Christmas. "A fine soldier."

This confirmed my assumption that he'd come from the faery fortress in the forest.

"She's done right by him." I heard the grudging respect in his voice, and I nodded my agreement. Mara made a fine mother.

He changed tack. "My real name Cleon Philbert Grizzle. Everyone calls me Grizzle though. I suppose you can too, but I'd prefer it if you didn't tell your gung-ho police friends."

I tipped my head at him. "I'll never tell them anything you're not happy for me to share." I pushed the final piece of orange cake his way. "Did you kill the woman we found in the forest?"

"Cah!" Grizzle made a strange noise as though he were half-choking, half-laughing. "Why don't you come straight out with it, oh-witchy-acquaintance-of-mine. You're very direct, aren't you?"

"Alf. My name is Alf," I reminded him. "Did you?"

"No I did not. How would a faery my size fell a human of that size?" He pointed at me. "Take you! You'd crush me half to death if you sat on me."

I frowned. "I'd crush you *all* the way to death, mate. There's no need to be rude."

"Whatever," he waved my emotions away as an

inconsequence. "I didn't kill her. She was dead when I came upon her."

"And when was that?" I asked, suddenly remembering the eyes I'd seen in the foliage.

Grizzle ducked his head and busied himself with the crumbs on the plate.

"You were there when I found her, weren't you?" I couldn't help the note of triumph in my voice. "You ran away. Why did you bother coming back to the scene? You could have just stayed away; the police would have been none the wiser."

He shrugged, still not meeting my eyes. "I didn't know where I was. I must have walked in a circle."

"Mmm." I wasn't buying it, but I didn't want to probe too deeply now that we'd finally started talking. "You could have just gone back to the fortress. You can't have been that lost."

"I didn't want to go back." Now Grizzle did meet my eyes. He lifted his chin in defiance. "I left the fortress for good reasons."

"Oh?" My curiosity was now well and truly piqued. "Why?"

Grizzle licked his finger and stuck in into the centre of the granules in the sugar bowl.

"Because I'm sick to the back teeth of hearing about Christmas. It's all Christmas this and

Christmas that and I hate it. Hate it. Hate it. Hate it!"

I recoiled from his vitriol. "How can you possibly hate Christmas? Nobody hates Christmas."

"Well I do!"

"I'm sorry to hear that."

"Are you? Are you really? I doubt that you genuinely are if the truth be known." He braced himself to begin a rant. "There's plenty of evidence downstairs that you're celebrating this infernal time of year too. Just like everybody else."

"Well I have a duty to my guests," I tried to explain. "Some of us celebrate Yule and some celebrate Christmas. It's all the same to me. Lots of food and drink; fires and candles. I like to keep everything cosy—"

"Cosy schmosy. It's a veneer of gentility and compassion. Total nonsense."

"But everyone is so lovely to each other and it makes you feel good—" I tried to explain.

"It's ridiculous," Grizzle exploded. "Everyone pretends to like everyone else for five minutes and then by the end of December they all end up as grumpy as they were before. The arguments start. People are rude to each other. The world becomes a negative and hate filled place once more. Come January all the goodwill is forgotten."

"I think that's a little harsh."

"And all that tat. Decorations. Baubles. Present wrapping. I hate it!"

"You've said." I shifted backwards out of the way of his ire. "I love it."

"And why red and green?" He ignored me. "Why is everything red and green?"

"Well I suppose those are the colours we most associate with December. Pine trees, holly and red berries?"

"Total rot. Most of the trees in Whittle Forest are devoid of leaves and the berries have all been and gone. The natural world isn't red and green at this time of year. It's brown and muddy and grey and white."

He kind of had a point, although I didn't consider 'muddy' a colour by itself.

"And besides those are elf colours. I hate elves. I hate red and green. Yuck!"

"Fair enough." I held my hands up in surrender. "I'm sorry I asked."

"But not sorry enough to take down your decorations, I'll warrant."

I pursed my lips. "No. You're right, I'm not sorry

enough to do that. I have other guests to consider after all." I couldn't resist adding, "Paying ones."

Grizzle made a snorting noise. "I can be out of your way in no time at all, oh-witchy-one. I'll just resume my hunt for somewhere to stay in the forest." He leered at me, a crafty look crossing his features. "Perhaps Mara would consider taking me in."

"No, no." I replied quickly. "Don't you go upsetting her." The last thing I needed was another winter storm to ruin my festivities like last year. "You're welcome to stay here for as long as you need. And you don't have to spend any time downstairs if you don't want to. We can have meals brought up here to you."

"Cake."

"Pardon?"

Grizzle smiled. "Not meals. I don't need those. Just cake."

"That's hardly a balanced diet," I retorted, although I did of course have some sympathy with his dietary requirements.

Grizzle capitulated. "And pastries. Maybe the odd savoury pie."

I nodded. "Florence makes a mean pie."

"And I'm free to come and go as I please?" Grizzle checked.

"Of course," I said in surprise. "You're not my prisoner."

Grizzle jumped up and then with some difficulty pulled himself onto the bed and lay back against the pillows. He looked tiny against them.

"Good."

I stood to take my leave. As I placed my fingers on the door handle, somebody walked along the corridor outside.

"Whachee! Whachee! Whachee!"

"Is there nothing you can do about all that noise?" Grizzle looked irritated.

I sighed. "I told you. We're working on it."

"Jolly good." He folded his arms across his chest. "Because once you've sorted that minor issue out, I'm certain Whittle Inn will be the perfect abode for me." He grinned at me. "Why, I may never leave!"

Chapter Eight

"What's up, boss?"

We'd finished the breakfast service and I'd retired to the kitchen for a strong coffee and a bacon butty. Florence was working like a trojan, making final preparations for her cake display, while several of my other ghosts attended to loading the dishwasher and cleaning up after Monsieur Emietter's egg-frying, poaching and scrambling bonanza. Charity plonked herself down beside me on the bench. I'd evidently been staring into space for a few minutes because my tea was cool and the fat starting to congeal on my bacon. I looked sideways at her. She was twirling a lock of hair around her finger. I finally realised she'd changed her hair colour. It was now Grinch green.

"I thought you were dying your hair yellow?"

"Oh I thought you hadn't noticed." Charity

winked at me. "I suggested yellow to my hairdresser, but she gave me a flat out 'no'. She said it would make me look washed out at this time of year. Apparently after a few weeks, lemon yellow can have a tendency to look like you've tried to dye it blonde on the cheap because the roots start to show again. So I opted for this perennial Christmas favourite instead." She fluffed up the spikes on the top of her head. "What do you think?"

I didn't hesitate. "I love it. I agree with your hairdresser that yellow wouldn't have looked right, especially this close to Christmas."

"Great minds then." Charity nodded in satisfaction. "I think it's nice to make an effort in honour of the festivities, don't you?"

I regarded her with uncertainty for a moment. Was she suggesting that I hadn't made an effort and probably wouldn't? Or was she simply generalising? I decided on the latter, grunting my assent, and changed the subject quickly. "Do you like Christmas, Charity?"

"I do. It's fun. Even when you're working. Which we will be of course." She threw me a little side-eye. "Everyone wants to have a good time, so it's not like real work."

I nodded and fiddled with my bacon until she elbowed me. "Why? Don't you like it?"

"Yes. I love Yule and I love Christmas. The same as you. I love the warmth and good feeling. I enjoy the gathering together of friends and family." My thoughts turned to Grizzle. How could he not feel the same way? I felt a little sad for him.

I mentioned him to Charity. "The faery that George brought here yesterday? He doesn't like Christmas?"

"Gandalf? Perhaps it's an occupational hazard for faeries," Charity smirked. "Maybe they don't appreciate the idea of being stuck on the top of a Christmas tree with a branch inserted where the sun doesn't shine."

My mouth dropped open and I stared at her in shock. She wiggled her eyebrows, Groucho Marx style, and then we both fell about laughing.

"Please don't say that in front of him," I said when I could manage to control myself.

"Well what's his problem? What's not to like? Presents, food, drink, Christmas songs, rubbish TV, games, good company?"

"The shine in people's eyes," I added.

"Yes!" Charity ejaculated. "Shining eyes and hearts full of love. Peace on earth and goodwill to all men, women, witches, faeries and others." She shook her head in amazement. "How can a faery not see the magic of the festive season?"

Charity had hit the nail on the head. Perhaps Grizzle didn't recognise the magick inherent in the season?

I would have to make it my mission to show him differently.

"Whoop! Mind how you go, Miss Alf."

I stepped backwards, only narrowly missing colliding with a three-tiered cake currently flying through the air and heading along the corridor towards the bar.

"Sorry Florence," I apologised. "I should have been watching where I was going. What time are the photographers here?"

"I'm expecting them at midday or thereabouts. They're coming down from London." Florence took control of the cake, and successfully navigated the final door. I followed her through and watched as she parked it—expertly—on one of the smaller round tables. This cake, a proper fruited Christmas cake had to be the central attraction. The icing was as smooth as a baby's bottom, as white as snow and perfect in every way. Florence had created a Father Christmas on a sleigh full to the brim of presents to decorate the top tier. On the bottom two tiers, a series of wrapped presents had been scattered seemingly at random, and there were little tiny hoof prints in the snow.

"Oh it's gorgeous." I leaned over it to take a better look at the intricate piping, but Florence wafted me away.

"You just step away from that cake, Miss Alf. No offence but this one took me weeks. I won't be able to do it again."

"Are you suggesting I'm clumsy?" I asked as I reversed away, backing into one of the other tables and making the crockery jiggle.

Florence levelled me with a serious gaze. "Certainly not, Miss Alf. I don't know why you'd say that."

She flitted over to where I had now parked myself—out of harm's way—and began to straighten up the table. Another white cake, but I recognised this one as her fabulous carrot and raisin cake with cream cheese frosting. She'd surrounded it with a circle of tiny plates, each of which had a carrot neatly piped on to it, now waiting to receive a slice of Florence's fabulous and fruity deliciousness.

"Sorry," I said, when she had everything rearranged to her satisfaction.

She wiggled her fingers at me. "Don't worry, miss. I'm feeling a little spaced out myself today. It must be all the excitement. I've been quite the butterfingers. I made some little choux pastry Brussel sprouts decorated in green, but I dropped them all over the floor."

"Choux pastry sprouts? They sound… interesting."

"Oh I have it on good authority from Frau Krauss that they're wunderbar." She smiled. "Although to be fair she prefers my kirsch chocolate bombs the most."

"Why have I not tried those?" I demanded.

Florence gestured at a different table. "After all the photographs have been taken today, you may have what you like, Miss Alf, but you need to remember to leave some for our guests too."

"I will." I pouted. "I don't know why I have this reputation as a glutton—"

Florence held her hand up suddenly, a look of alarm crossing her pretty young face.

"What's the matter?" I asked.

She shook her head and wrinkled her nose, waving me away.

"Florence?" I asked in alarm.

She seemed to struggle for breath. Her mouth opened in a grimace and then—

"*Yachee.*" A timorously quiet sneeze.

"Bless you," I said.

"*Yachee.*"

"Bless you again."

"*Yachee.*"

Oh no. Not today of all days.

"*Yachee. Yachee. Yachee.*"

"Florence. I think you may have caught—"

"No!" Florence's roar reminded me of the demon's voice in *The Exorcist*; a film I'd watched as a young teenager and never again since. "I can't afford to be ill."

"Perhaps—" I tried to think of something practical and soothing to say, but Florence had started making that juddering chest movement again. She swallowed and stopped. Then tipped her head back and flung it forwards.

"*Yacheeeeeeeeeeeooowa!*"

Quite simply, it was a tremendous sneeze. A sneeze—one would have hoped—that would end all sneezes. It probably registered on the Richter scale, and I was sure, without doubt, that the walls of the inn shook.

The drawback was that somehow—inexplicably—as Florence had sneezed, she had shaken soot all over the carrot cake and the plates on the table in front of us.

Her scream when she noticed what she'd done caused consternation throughout the inn. A few ghosts apparated into the bar to find out what had happened, and I heard the doors of several guest rooms open on the floor directly above us. "What?" she shrieked. "Who has done this to me? Who has made me ill?"

"Calm down, Florence." I tried to placate her. "We'll get this cleaned up. It will all be fine."

"Whachee!"

"Bless you—"

"I'll kill them! I'll bury a machete in their head. A cake knife in their chest. A... a... meat cleaver through their testicles. It was Luppitt, wasn't it? I'll kill him. I will!"

"Florence!" Alarmed, I waved my hands at her, trying to distract her from the cake. I could just imagine the trauma if she attacked poor Luppitt given his long history of repeated deaths.

"Yachee!" She shook with emotion. "Why today?

The photographers are coming! I need to be well! *Yachee!*"

I couldn't handle this situation on my own. Charity had now poked her head around the door but having ascertained the problem she seemed loath to wade in and help me. "Grandmama?" I called.

"Yachee. It's the end of my career, Miss Alf! After all my work."

"I think you're being a little melodramatic, Florence," I soothed. "Grandmama?"

"And what about all the preparations for Yule? It's just a few days away. *Yachee!*"

"Stop worrying. We'll sort it." Where was Gwyn? "Grandmama?"

Then she was there. "Florence? My dear girl. You're as white as a sheet." She took the housekeeper by the arm and slowly pulled her away. "Have you been taken ill as well? Stop making such a fuss. You'll be right as rain in a few days."

"You don't understand," Florence wailed as the pair apparated away. I caught the words, 'photographers' and 'Yule' and 'Christmas' and then peace was restored to the bar.

I gazed down at the ruined carrot cake. Could I somehow rectify it?

I went to pick the plate up, intending to carry it

through to the kitchen and try and ask Monsieur Emietter's opinion on salvaging the cake, when out of nowhere came a tiny hand. It reached out and ripped off a huge chunk from the side.

Grizzle.

He stuffed the cake in his mouth and reached for more.

"Hey!" I scolded him.

"Nice," he managed to say, his mouth full and his eyes shining with merriment. "Very tasty."

CHAPTER NINE

"Now is really not the best time," I grumbled, as I joined George outside the small café in Whittlecombe. I huddled inside my long coat. There was a nasty nip in the air and my cheeks were numb with cold. The inside of the café glowed with warmth; the windows steamed up. I could just about make out human shapes inside. "Can we go in?" I slapped my hands together to warm them up. I'd unintentionally left my mittens at home, along with my wand and my purse.

"I had to come out here to interview someone about a suspicious sighting in the forest. I figured I'd kill two birds with one stone," George said.

"Well pity us poor birds," I replied, and without further ado marched inside the café. The little bell above the door tinkled as we entered, and Gloria, who had been a waitress here for several decades waved us an acknowledgement.

"Take a seat, DS Gilchrist. I'll be right with you." Gloria bustled about with teacups and saucers at the serving counter near the kitchen. I chose a table and plonked myself down. The café was beautifully warm, and I could feel myself defrosting, but I still wasn't keen to take my coat off just yet.

George took the seat opposite me and pulled out his notebook and pen.

"Are you interviewing me again?" I asked.

"Potentially."

"Do I need a lawyer?" I asked, sounding as cranky as I felt.

George looked amused. "What's got your knickers in a twist?"

"Oh. You know. This and that." I exhaled for a long while and rolled my shoulders back. "I'm having one of those weeks. The inn is at capacity, half of my ghosts have the flu, and I'm babysitting a faery for you. Not to mention—" I waved my finger at him, "—the murder of one of my guests."

"I—"

"And!" I hadn't finished. "I have some photographers on their way from London to take photos of all of Florence's cakes for inclusion in her baking book, but this morning Florence was taken unexpectedly ill herself, and she sneezed soot all over one of the cakes. Then she had a meltdown. Meanwhile, my great-grandmother is pretending to be Florence Nightingale in the attic." I nodded at Gloria who had just arrived at our table. "Other than that, I'm fine and dandy. Feed me a hot scone, George and I might just forgive you for dragging me out in sub-zero temperatures."

"Don't exaggerate," George responded. "It's not that cold."

I rolled my eyes and studied the specials board.

George smiled at Gloria, intent on charming her. "Please may I have a cup of your finest coffee, and a great stodgy sausage sandwich?"

"Brown sauce, DS Gilchrist?" Gloria asked. She obviously knew his preferences only too well.

"Aye. Thank you. And my friend here will have a hot chocolate with whipped cream and marshmallows and a warm cheese scone." I pulled a face at him. And he knew me too well.

"Thank you," I said grudgingly, watching as Gloria ambled back towards the kitchen to deliver our order.

"My pleasure. I hope it goes some way to making up for dragging you away from the chaos at the inn."

"You could have just come up there to visit me."

"You're always so busy. And besides, I wanted to avoid Gandalf." George cocked an eyebrow. "How is he?"

I snorted like a horse. "Boy that faery has an appetite, but only for sweet things. I had to put Charity on guard in case he ate all of Florence's cakes before the photographers arrive. Needless to say, his name is not Gandalf, but at the moment I don't have permission to share his real name with you."

George frowned. "Permission?"

"Yes, DS Gilchrist. I'm not shopping him, even for you." I tapped my fingers on the table. Service in the café was normally pretty swift, but today, aware of how little time I had available, I gave in to my impatience.

"Did he murder Linda?" George asked the most important question and I shook my head, my face grave.

"I'd say no. Definitely not. He was there when I found the body though, I'm fairly certain of that. So he might have seen something, although he says he didn't." I shrugged. "But I believe him when he says he had nothing to do with her death."

"I thought as much." George groaned. "But that

puts me back to square one. I have no leads. And a plane to catch in a few days."

"What about this demon creature with flaming red eyes that everyone in the village is talking about?" I asked as Gloria arrived at the table with our drinks and my scone. "Could there be some truth to that?"

"Your sandwich won't be long, DS Gilchrist," Gloria told him, flushing a little pink. He beamed his thanks.

I leaned over to inhale the steam from my scone. Cheesy heaven.

"I think this creature only exists in people's imaginations." George watched me.

I picked up my knife and sliced into the scone, releasing a fresh cloud of pungent mist. "Quite a few people claim to have seen it."

"Have they b—"

"Here's your sandwich, DS Gilchrist. I've added extra sauce just the way you like it." Gloria appeared at George's elbow and set his doorstopper sandwich down. It did look good.

"You're an angel, Gloria. A true gem. Thank you. I'll let Father Christmas know you've been a good girl."

The waitress toddled away with a peal of merry laughter. Gloria appeared to be sweet on the DS.

I took a mouthful of scone and chewed happily, savouring it. "So you're saying the monster in the woods doesn't exist?"

"I am saying that, yes," George confirmed. "It's more likely some form of mass hysteria." He cut through his sandwich with some difficulty. "I'm also poo-pooing the notion that she was killed by a monster at all. We don't have a definitive cause of death yet, but she wasn't pulled limb from limb by any kind of animal."

"What then?" I nibbled on a chunk of scone.

George shrugged. "There's a head injury. A fractured skull. But I'm not sure it's serious enough to account for her death. We'll know more in a day or two." He waved his knife at me. "That's strictly between us."

"Have you found anything out about her? Where she lived?"

"Well you gave us an address for her, and our colleagues in London have paid the flat a visit, but so far that hasn't yielded much information. What did she do while she was with you at the inn?"

I thought back. "Nothing much. She just went out on walks. Sat alone for breakfast and dinner and didn't really engage in conversation. She read a book occasionally. Avoided chatting to the other guests."

"Anti-social would you say?"

I shook my head. "Not really. Just... self-contained."

"And these walks? Where did she go?"

"I don't know. I'm assuming, because she was found in the forest, that she liked the wildlife and scenery." I hadn't really given it much thought. "She was dressed for the elements, wasn't she?"

"Kind of. She didn't have walking boots or socks on, but she did have an expensive windcheater. That seems a bit odd to me."

"So not a seasoned walker then?"

"Difficult to tell." George bit into his sandwich.

"Did you find her handbag? Purse? Anything that could help?"

"Nothing at all." George chewed and swallowed. "I've a couple of officers out there in the forest searching for her bag, but so far they haven't located anything fresh. It's like looking for a needle in a haystack at this time of year. The leaves have covered everything."

"I'll tell my guests to keep an eye out if they're wandering through Speckled Wood."

George fixed me with a canny eye. "Maybe you

should ask Mr Hoo to have a look-see when he's out and about. He'd make a great detective."

"Alright, I'll do that." I finished up my scone and took a large gulp of my hot chocolate. "I really need to go, I'm afraid. Can't keep the bigwigs from London waiting, can I?"

"Certainly not. If you want to wait a minute, I'll give you a lift back."

I regarded the enormous plate of sausage and bread George still had to wade through. "Don't give yourself indigestion," I said. "It'll be quicker if I run."

Typically the photographers turned up late, their taxi driver having lost his way from Exeter, but once in situ, and having been fortified by refreshments, they proved professional and efficient. They set up a 'mini studio' with a white cloth background and some bright lights. Each cake was then placed centrally and photographed from numerous angles.

Florence probably wouldn't have approved, but the creative director of photography—a lovely young graduate named Mia—happily staged the photos using a variety of different props, including flowers and Christmas decorations, soft toys for the child's christening cake, party hats for her birthday cakes, and pillar candles for Florence's replica Halloween showcase. She kept asking me for my opinion, but everything looked wonderful to me, so I don't imagine I provided any assistance whatsoever.

Florence had put a great deal of effort into setting up the tables, but she needn't have worried at all because it hadn't been required. I watched the photographers at work, thinking about my poor housekeeper, stuck as she was in the attic, submitting to the ministrations of my bossy great-grandmother. I felt guilty, as though I were somehow to blame for the bad timing of the flu outbreak. One thing was for certain, I needed to locate the doctor that Perdita had recommended, and I needed to do it soon. But how could I find the time, this close to all the festive celebrations?

The sound of sneezing coming from upstairs tugged at my heart strings. Florence was missing all of this. "Do you mind if I take some photos?" I asked Mia, intending to show them to my housekeeper later.

"Of course not. I'm so sorry Florence couldn't be here today. I was so looking forward to meeting her. I've never met a ghost before."

I smiled. I could have taken a moment to point

out the ghost light of her grandfather who was following her around like a faithful hound, but I decided to hold my tongue.

"She's gutted to miss you," I told her instead, and snapped away with my mobile phone. I would download hard copies from my computer this evening and visit Florence in the attic. As long as Gwyn allowed visitors, that is.

Her ward, her rules, I imagined.

"We'll need to do a cover photo at some stage," Mia reminded me, and I winced a little. How would that go? Given Florence's general appearance. Mia grinned at my reaction. "Oh don't worry, after the success of *The Great Witchy Cake Off*, I think everyone knows what Florence looks like, there'll be no great surprise there. I think it's wonderful that so many people, the world over, took her to their hearts in spite of her appearance, don't you?"

"I do," I said. "I'm frightened she's going to run away to Hollywood or somewhere."

Mia laughed. "I suppose there's a very real possibility that that could happen. She was a natural on the screen."

I nodded, my stomach sinking. *Don't leave me, Florence*, I was thinking.

"Perhaps you could escort her up to London?" Mia suggested. "It would be a fun day out."

I recalled the day we'd tramped around the Isle of Dogs searching for someone to help us solve a computer issue. That someone had ended up being Ross Baines. Yes. That had been a marvellously fun day.

Not.

"I'll certainly give that some thought," I replied.

CHAPTER TEN

The photographers left at just before six, intent on catching the 7 pm train from Exeter to Paddington. That would get them home in time for bed. It gave Charity and I less than an hour to prepare the bar for the dinner service. Keeping a sharp eye out for greedy Grizzle, I co-opted an assortment of ghosts to help me carry the cakes down the back passage, through the kitchen and into the large cold stores out the back. Once everything was safely stored away, I organised a table setting crew. Silverware and our best glassware flew through the air, down the hall and back into the bar, where tablecloths were hastily thrown over the wooden tables, and places marked out.

Without Florence to hand, the task of double checking everything fell to me. Charity brought out wine and baskets of bread and olives for our Italian themed evening, while Ned prepared the bar itself; slicing lemons and filling the ice bucket.

The phone behind the bar rang and Charity who was closest took the call. When she hung up, she turned to me. "That was Grizzle. He said to let you know he's hungry."

"Did he really?" I glowered. "How can he possibly be hungry? He polished off a whole carrot cake earlier on. I'd have thought he'd be lying in a diabetic coma somewhere by now."

"Well, he asked for dessert." Charity smirked at me and I laughed, tickled at the idea of eating dessert after only eating pudding in the first place.

"Cheeky blighter! I'll see to it," I said when I could breathe again. "You just supervise dinner."

She nodded and disappeared down the passage towards the kitchen as the phone rang again. Thinking it would be Grizzle complaining about a lack of instant cake gratification I picked it up. "I'm coming," I told him.

Except it wasn't Grizzle.

"How did you know I was going to ask you to?" asked a familiar female voice.

"Millicent?"

"Yes. Are you reading minds now, Alf? That's a marvellous skill. It will save me having to call you via the landline. I did try your mobile first." That was still upstairs by my bed. Along with my wand of course. Would I ever learn? I could almost sense Silvan's disapproval.

"I thought you were someone else," I stated the obvious. "Were you really going to suggest I come down into the village?" This wasn't an appealing thought. It had been dark for a few hours and I had no doubt the temperature had dropped close to freezing outside. Plus, I was nice and warm here inside the inn.

"Yes, actually."

I grimaced. "I'm a bit tied up at the moment. We're just about to start serving dinner."

"Now, Alf. You know I wouldn't suggest you came down here unless I felt it was important. It's just that Gladstone Talbot-Lloyd—"

Talbot-Lloyd. The wealthiest landowner in the area. The man who had always had designs on the grounds that Whittle Inn inhabited. We'd had several confrontations in the past. "Oh no. What's he up to now?"

"He's called a village meeting. It's due to start at half-past seven. He wants to take a team of locals into the forest to hunt down the monster with red eyes."

"But... George said there was no monster."

"Talbot-Lloyd disagrees."

"Evidently." I chewed the inside of my cheek, thinking quickly. We were already short-staffed, but Charity would just have to cope. It wouldn't be the first time. The thought of Talbot-Lloyd hanging out where he wasn't wanted, especially anywhere close to Speckled Wood had me feeling incredibly insecure.

I made my mind up.

"I'm on my way."

As village meetings went this was not the best attended, primarily because the temperature had dipped below freezing. As I huffed my way down into the village, for the second time that day, my breath blew out of me in big steamy gasps, and the vehicles parked along the lane sparkled with the early formation of frost particles.

Squeezing between the cars, I resisted the urge to draw love hearts on the glass of the Jeeps and Range Rovers parked on double yellow lines outside the Village Hall. Instead I burst in through the rickety wooden door, disturbing the meeting that had started five minutes before. Everyone turned around to get a look at the tardy latecomer and I smiled bashfully. Fortunately, Millicent was sitting at the rear, close to the door. I sidled along her row and plopped down into my seat, cringing as it creaked and created a further disturbance.

From the stage at the front Gladstone Talbot-Lloyd directed a withering scowl my way. Of course he wouldn't be happy I was here. I peered over the heads in front of me. Lyle Cavendish, landlord of The Hay Loft had taken pride of place in the front row. The remaining audience made up from the usual assortment of locals. For the most part these were busybodies with too little to do of an evening, and a number of worried younger people in their twenties and early thirties, whom I assumed were parents.

"Glad you could make it," Millicent whispered.

"I'd hardly miss it. In my absence they'd have probably framed me for the murder *and* decided they wanted to hang, draw and quarter me. I thought I'd better put in an appearance."

The woman in front of me turned and gave me 'a look'. The sort of passive aggressive glare you give someone at the cinema when they eat their snacks too loudly or start talking into their phone. I offered a thin smile and settled back in my seat to listen to Talbot-Lloyd's bluff and bluster.

"It's an obvious concern for everyone in the village," he was saying.

A man a few rows from the front put his hand up and Talbot-Lloyd nodded at him. "Trevor? Did you want to say something?"

The man named Trevor cleared his throat. "I did as it happens." He stood up. "Only, I've heard the rumours about this beast but so far we've only one or two semi-credible witnesses. With all due respect, I'm not sure these accounts amount to much more than folk tales really. I think we may be getting a bit ahead of ourselves."

I nodded. *Tell it like it is, Trev*, I thought.

"What do the police have to say about all this?" Trevor continued. "Have you approached them?"

Trevor took his seat and Talbot-Lloyd nodded in all seriousness. "You make valid points there, Trevor. I did ask the police to attend this evening, but unfortunately they have other more pressing matters to attend to, apparently."

I bristled on George's behalf. Of course he had other things to do. He couldn't be everywhere at once, could he?

"Isn't it true they've dismissed the idea of a beast

in the forest?" One young woman asked. "I mean, shouldn't we take them at their word?" There was a general mumbling in the hall; some spectators in agreement and others not so much.

Talbot-Lloyd held up his hands. "Order, order, please." When the audience had quietened down once more, he continued, "The fact remains that we *do* have two *credible* sightings from villagers of the Whittle Beast." He looked pointedly at Trevor.

I couldn't help myself, I laughed out loud. I wasn't alone, some others joined in, but it was to me whom Talbot-Lloyd directed a glare of sheer poison.

"That's the most ridiculous thing I've ever heard," I said, but he was already moving on.

"I don't think we can dismiss the experiences of the victims, can we, Ms Daemonne? Not at the expense of the landowners—like yourself—who may well be sued for inaction if they have dangerous animals roaming around their property."

That shut me up.

"To give some context to the matter I've invited Sarah Corby to tell us what happened to her." He gestured at a woman sitting alongside Lyle Cavendish in the front row.

She stood at his invitation and turned to face us. I recognised her as the woman whom I'd seen rushing along Whittle Lane after I'd visited the post office a few days before. I listened with interest as she launched into her tale of woe.

"I'd been walking along the path that leads towards Whittle Folly when something caught my eye," she recounted. She tugged at the scarf wound around her neck, as though it had started to suffocate her. "I could hear something in the bushes. At first, I wasn't worried, because you hear lots of creatures up there when you're walking... birds and what have you. But I carried on walking and it followed me. I couldn't see it and it sounded quite large. I was a bit scared because... well you know... I was on my own."

She swallowed and finally pulled her scarf free, folding and unfolding it as she resumed talking. "I couldn't see anything and after walking ten or so metres I stopped and called out, to see who it was. There was no reply and the noise stopped and I carried on walking. I wasn't far from the scout hut at that stage."

"So did you see it or not?" Someone asked, a little rudely. For my part I hung on tenterhooks.

Sarah flushed. "When I started walking once more, the noise came again. It sounded like something trampling through the bushes. I turned and I saw this thing—" she dropped her scarf and held out her hands, wide apart. "This enormous thing... and it had horns and its eyes were raging!" She shuddered, close to tears.

"It had horns?" I asked. "Doesn't that sound like a stag?" A few people nodded.

"Exactly!" Trevor said. "Nothing sinister about it at all."

"It was angry!" Sarah Corby reiterated.

"Did it really have red eyes?" The woman in front of me asked. "Because deer don't have red eyes."

"Maybe it was a trick of the light," Trevor suggested.

Pockets of people started to discuss what had been said and the noise levels in the hall rose again. "Order! Order!" called Talbot-Lloyd. "I think the facts are clear—"

"They definitely aren't." I folded my arms in defiance, but he ignored me.

"There *is* something out there in Whittle Forest. I am proposing that we need a search party to go out and hunt it down." There were murmurs of agreement and groans of disagreement. "What I'm suggesting is that we form a hunting party and head out into the forest in small groups."

"A hunting party?" I called out, trying to make

myself heard above the general hubbub. "You're going to shoot it? With guns?"

"Well they're not going to shoot it with cameras, are they?" The woman in front of me retorted.

I stared open-mouthed as Talbot-Lloyd called for order again. "If we have any farmers or anyone with a gun license who would care to join us, make yourself known. We'll get started this evening."

"This is preposterous," Millicent said.

"That can't be legal, surely?" I asked her. "They can't just go into the forest and shoot at anything that moves. There must be laws against that. This is England, not the Wild West."

The meeting was beginning to break up. Most people were shaking their heads and leaving Talbot-Lloyd and his gung-ho band of brothers—because there were no female volunteers—to it. I made my way to the front of the hall and tried to break through the group of men surrounding him, but he studiously avoided all my attempts to speak with him.

I marched back to Millicent, hovering at the rear of the hall. Her forehead had creased in consternation and she regarded me with concern. "What are you going to do?" she asked.

"Well first things first I'm going to give George a ring. I'm pretty sure he still has officers in the woods searching for evidence. I haven't heard that they've withdrawn yet." I fished my mobile from my coat pocket. "But in any case, he needs to know that there will be armed idiots on the loose in Whittlecombe tonight." I thumbed the screen and quickly located George's number. "It may be December and it may be freezing out there, but anyone could be in the forest and someone could be seriously hurt. We can't have that on our consciences."

CHAPTER ELEVEN

"It's always nice to have a little company," Finbarr announced cheerfully as I told him I'd be joining him on his foray into Speckled Wood that evening.

"It's not for a chinwag and bonfire jamboree," I said, pulling on my walking boots and struggling with the laces.

"Ah, now. I didn't for a minute imagine it would be that simple." He winked.

"I'm not sure it's going to be simple at all." I cursed at my laces. They were mud encrusted and my fingers were cold. I seemed to have lost the dexterity I needed to secure my boots.

Finbarr pulled out his wand. "*Ligare!*" he said.

The shoelaces slipped through my fingers and tied themselves in neat bows. "You'll need to wrap up warm there, Alf. It's colder than—"

"I know. I've only just come back from the village." I wished heartily for Florence's presence. She would have filled up a thermos with hot chocolate or tea and we could have taken that with us. I didn't really want to stop and make a flask myself. Time was of the essence.

"I've leggings on underneath my trousers," I said. "And a vest, a t-shirt and two jumpers. Do you think that will be enough?"

"Thermal vest?" Finbarr looked at me with incredulity and I nodded. I'd learned my lesson about proper outdoor clothes last Christmas when I'd been entirely unprepared for the winter conditions in the forest. This year I'd invested in proper clothing. I now had a warm, windproof coat to wear. I shrugged it on, zipped it up and buttoned down the flaps. For his part, Finbarr didn't seem to feel the cold, but then given that he was out in it overnight, every night, come rain or snow, I expected he'd acclimatised.

I patted my pockets. Torch, wand and mobile phone. Not that I'd be likely to have much of a signal once we ventured into the woods proper, but you could never know when a phone might come in handy. If I'd had one the night I'd found Linda's body, I wouldn't have had to run back to the inn to summon assistance. Fortunately—or unfortunately—depending on your take on such things, she had been well beyond help.

I pulled my hat down over my ears. "Let's go," I said and waddled out of the back door, the weight of all the excess clothing constraining my movements.

Finbarr followed me. "Would you be telling me what we're about this fine evening?"

"Talbot-Lloyd is searching for the Beast of Whittle Forest," I told him as he fell in beside me and started to match my stride.

"There's a Beast?" Finbarr asked. "That's news to me."

I sniffed. "I think the whole thing is made up. But whatever it is, it has all the local landowners and farmers out with their guns tonight. They're searching for this 'creature' whatever it may be, and no doubt they will shoot on sight if they find it or anything even remotely resembling it."

"I'm certain that if there was anything in the forest that shouldn't be, we would know about it," Finbarr said. "I'd have seen some evidence of it, or the pixies would have, and they would have told me."

"That's my thinking too. And George's. I phoned him to let him know what Talbot-Lloyd is up to."

"Ah that's grand, then. There'll be no unsuspecting boys-in-blue caught unawares."

"Or girls. Except there probably will be at some stage. George is sending a party to apprehend Talbot-Lloyd's hunters. They have no license to be out here at this time of night looking to shoot things. The police will warn them off."

"If they don't go?"

"I suppose there will be a few arrests."

We'd made it to the edge of Speckled Wood. Above us, the branches on the trees, skeletal and stark against the sky, shone with frost.

"So, it's going to be busy out here tonight. To be sure the sheer levels of noise will frighten anything off that's trying to hide out or even just get a decent night's kip." He paused and looked at me. "Remind me. Just what are we going to be doing out here ourselves, might I ask?"

From overhead came the rhythmic beating of large wings. Mr Hoo settled into a tree nearby and stared down at me with bright orange eyes. I saluted him. "We're going to locate the Beast of Whittle Forest before anyone else does."

"Right." Finbarr considered this. "And if we do find this Beastie, what are we going to do then?"

"We're going to ask him what he wants, of course."

Finbarr knew Speckled Wood inside out. He could probably have circumnavigated it with his eyes closed. The earth itself had frozen; hard and unyielding. Although the floor of the forest had been coated in fallen leaves, pinecones and chestnut cases. If we did have any trips or stumbles, they would make for a softer landing. By following my little Irish friend, I avoided all the pitfalls I might have stumbled across in the dark had I been alone; the badger holes, the mini ravines, the trees that had been felled by storms.

We made our way slowly and carefully towards the boundary of my land. If you knew where to look you would easily spot the forcefield that burned like a wall of electric ribbon thanks to its bright glow. It appeared healthy to me, uninterrupted, and Finbarr only gave it a cursory glance as we approached it.

Above us, Mr Hoo continued to circle the canopy. That he could do this so silently seemed wondrous to me. No field mouse or shrew would have stood a chance had the owl been hunting. For now however, he searched for any sign of the Beast of Whittle Forest.

We paused at the forcefield and Mr Hoo settled high in the branches above us, his head turned to the south, towards Whittlecombe.

"What do you reckon?" Finbarr asked, keeping his voice low.

"I think we should go on, as though we were heading for the village," I whispered. "If we continue in this general direction it will take us towards Whittle Folly, right?"

"Eventually. More or less." Finbarr nodded. "I don't know the area beyond here so well, and we have strayed from the main paths."

"One of the villagers claimed to have been almost at the scout hut when she spotted this creature."

In the far distance the sound of a rifle shot made us both jump. "Bejesus." Finbarr said. "Thank the good Grandfather-of-Leprechauns that they're a way away."

"Mmm." I tilted my head, listening but we there were no more shots. "Sounds like they're still in Whittlecombe. Let's hope they stay there."

"Hooooo."

My owl called to me and I peered up, barely able

to make him out in the mute light. "See anything?" I called softly.

"Hooo. Hooooooo. Hooo-oooo."

"What's he saying?" Finbarr frowned. "Has he seen something?"

"Not seen but heard. Movement coming from the south. Heading this way."

"That would make sense if Talbot-Lloyd's men have scared something off."

My heart beat a little faster in my chest and we remained quiet; our ears, eyes and witch-senses straining, until Finbarr articulated what we were both thinking. "It could be the Beast."

"Yes." I considered our options. "We could... what is it that cowboys do? With horses and things when they round them up and one gets loose?"

"Corral?"

"Yes!" I smacked his arm. "We could corral him against the forcefield here."

"That's assuming he's going to head straight for us." Finbarr looked around. "He could always break off. Go left or right maybe."

"True." We'd need more than the two of us. Perhaps the pixies? I hurriedly discounted this idea and considered a few magickal options instead. Off the top of my head I wasn't sure I had any ensnarean-angry-forest-beast spells handy. I supposed in a worst-case scenario I could use a stun or an immobilise spell. I walked to my left, scouring the darkness but hearing nothing.

"You know, talking about corralling, back in the old country we're very laid back about horses and ponies." Finbarr's lyrical accent drifted after me. His accent always became broader, more lyrical, when he spoke about the land he loved.

"This isn't a horse though," I reminded him.

"But I'll wager the technique would be the same for whatever it is." Finbarr caught me up. "No animal can run forever. The hunting party are a way behind him. He'll come this way and not be able to make it through the forcefield. He'll have been running for a while. He'll slow down."

I stared at my little Irish friend; doubt gnawing away at my innards. "It's a theory."

"What do we have to lose?" Finbarr grinned at me, and without waiting for a response popped through the forcefield. After a moment, I followed suit.

"You'd better not be getting me killed," I said. "I've big plans for next year."

Finbarr gasped. "You're never in the world getting married there now, are you Alfhild?"

I reared back in shock. "By all that's green... No!" I gave Finbarr the evil eye. "I meant big plans for the inn."

"Oh. And there I was making the assumption you and Silvan would be jumping the broomstick."

"Certainly not," I replied, my tone prim. "We hardly know each other."

"You rub along very well for two people who don't know each other." Finbarr let out a guffaw that probably woke every non-nocturnal animal within a five-mile radius.

"Shhh!" I hissed.

We stood stock still and lapsed into silence; our ears straining to make out the slightest sound from anywhere. The cold seeped into my marrow and the sting of the icy air on my cheeks made my skin tingle.

"Hoooo." Mr Hoo alerted us to something coming closer. I hardly dared to breathe. I had to force myself to release the tension I'd been holding onto.

Then, "Hooooo," once more and the owl lifted from the tree, soaring gracefully up into the sky, sailing away from us.

"Where's he going?" Finbarr whispered.

I watched his direction of flight. "I don't know

but I think we should go after him, slowly and quietly."

Finbarr nodded and set off. I followed the Irish witch closely, knowing that stealth and silence were our watch words for now. We walked a little way until we re-joined a path. A bit further than that, I had a realisation. Police tape had been tied to a tree here, and although the scene had now been dismantled, several metres of it fluttered forlornly on the bitter breeze.

I reached out to tap Finbarr lightly on the back. He stopped. "We're near to where I found the woman last week," I whispered.

"Are you sure?"

I nodded and opened my mouth to say something else, when we heard the rapid clumping of cantering hooves on hard earth heading our way. Instantly my heart was in my mouth and my wand in my hand. Finbarr's too. We edged backwards, quietly, each of us taking shelter behind a tree. I jammed my back against the trunk and slunk to my knees, hugging the ground, as the sound of hooves grew louder.

The running slowed down to a trot and then a walk. There was a kind of snuffling noise, some snorting. 'It' had entered the little clearing. Clop

clop. The sound of hooves on rock. Then duller steps. Retreating.

I dared to twist my head to steal a look. Wand stretched ahead of me, I peered out from behind the tree expecting to see the Beast of Whittle Forest taking a breather.

Mist rose from the ground, catching the beams of moonlight that filtered down through the forest canopy. But of the beast?

There was no sign.

I gestured at Finbarr and he peeped out from behind his tree too. His head swivelled as he checked all around us, pointing his wand into the undergrowth, then looking back at me and shaking his head.

"Where did it go?" I pushed myself upright and walked towards the little clearing.

"Careful, Alf," Finbarr warned me.

"There's nothing to be afraid of here," I said. I glanced down at where I'd discovered the body of Linda Creary. No ghost light. She'd passed over. That was something.

The ground had been well trodden round here, the foliage cut down or beaten down by the police when they'd searched the area. I glanced back at where I'd seen the eyes watching me, Grizzle's eyes as it had turned out. Behind what had been a large holly bush was a rocky outcrop. Nothing unusual about that, here on the Jurassic coast where the forest eventually meets the sea, but unless my eyes were deceiving me there was a narrow gap in the rocks.

"Finbarr?" I pointed the rocks out to him, and we crept towards them. I extracted the torch from my pocket and pointed it towards the shadowy space.

"It's a cave of sorts," Finbarr said, edging up close to the entrance. I shone the torch inside the gap. The narrow entrance went on for some way and I experienced a sudden wave of claustrophobic terror.

"I'm not going in there. No way."

"I will." Finbarr reached out to take the torch from me.

I pulled it away from his hand. "Are you crazy? The Beast might be in there."

"Well we either sit here all night, freezing to death and hoping it will come out, or we go inside and make his acquaintance."

Or we could leave him to his own devices and hope he doesn't get himself shot by Talbot-Lloyd the trophy hunter, I thought.

None of these seemed to be appealing options. I sighed and held the torch out to Finbarr.

He gave me the thumbs up and accepted the torch from me. Holding it in one hand, and his wand in the other, he turned sideways and edged into the gap.

"Be careful," I said. "Don't make me come in there after you."

"Never fear. It'll all be fine," he said and disappeared.

He hadn't been gone more than a few seconds when I heard him cry out in surprise. I leaned my head into the gap to listen, my heart thumping like a jack hammer. I could see the faint trace of light where the passage turned a corner.

"Are you alright?" I called in alarm, and my voice reverberated along the narrow space.

"Pipe down, Alf. You're scaring him," came the response, his voice echoing crazily.

"I'm scaring him? Who is 'him'?"

"Easy, easy," I heard Finbarr say, and when I recognised the stomping of hooves once more, I could only assume he wasn't speaking to me. "Are you hungry?" Finbarr asked whatever it was. "What do you even eat? Not witches I hope?"

I hoped not too. Waiting for Finbarr to make an appearance, I hopped around. Partly from agitation and partly because the cold had started to get to me and I needed to warm up.

"Here we go, big fella. Come out now and meet your new stepmother."

I crinkled my nose. Stepmother? Had Finbarr been on the whisky before we ventured out this evening? I wouldn't put it past him.

"Alf? Would you do me a huge favour and just take hold of this lad's reins as he comes your way?"

Reins? Hooves? It was a horse then after all? I relaxed a little. I could handle a horse.

"Alright," I called back, and stood poised to make a grab as the animal headed out into the open.

But when the Beast emerged, I was so surprised, I forgot what I was doing and made no attempt to grab the reins at all, because this wasn't a horse at all. The horns kind of gave that away.

No, not a horse, but a reindeer.

And I do declare... He had a very shiny nose.

CHAPTER TWELVE

The reindeer regarded me with a bemused expression as I stood and gawped at it. He had glossy black eyes and the longest eyelashes I'd ever seen. And he was huge. I'd never realised how tall reindeer could grow. Including his antlers, he was easily as tall as me, possibly a little more.

His fur was kind of fleecy, a bit like a donkey I suppose. But it was his nose that stood out like a Belisha beacon, had Belisha beacons been habitually red and not yellow that is.

We stood and regarded each other in mutual curiosity. He made no attempt to walk off in spite of the fact that I'd forgotten to grab his harness.

"Do you think you could move your big backside out of the way, by any chance?" Finbarr's disembodied voice drifted out of the narrow entrance.

"Because I'm not getting out of here with you standing there, that's for sure."

"You'd better be referring to the reindeer and not to me," I growled, and tentatively reached out for the leather reins around the creature's neck. He didn't seem to mind though, and once I'd pulled him gently away from the cave, he seemed happy to walk alongside me.

Finbarr followed the reindeer out, scuffing his shoulder as he came. "Begorrah, it's tight in there even for me. How this big fella has been managing to go in and out I've no idea."

"He's tame," I said in wonder, stroking its forehead. "Did you see his nose, Finbarr?"

Finbarr moved alongside me. "Yes. It's red. How is it red?" He shone the torch full at the reindeer which backed away in alarm and nearly pulled me over in the process.

"Whoa!" I said, both to Finbarr and the horned creature at the end of my arm.

"Is it an injury, or does he have a red nose?" Finbarr lifted the torch once more, and annoyed I grabbed it from him.

"You're going to blind him if you keep shining that thing in his eyes."

"Maybe it is an injury," Finbarr repeated. "I've

had ponies that have scuffed their noses in the past. It will just need cleaning up."

"How long has he been living inside that cave I wonder?"

"Long enough, I think. Someone made a bed in there for him. It's all trampled down."

I patted the creature's flanks. "So he belongs to someone then?"

"I think the harness might be a giveaway," Finbarr agreed.

"And to be fair, reindeers are hardly native to Whittle woods, are they?" I flicked up the edges of the leather straps attached to the harness. "But see here? He's pulled free. These are ripped, not cut. If he was living here with his owner wouldn't they have replaced all this?"

Finbarr examined the leather straps more carefully. "You're right. So maybe someone has been looking after it recently, but they're not necessarily the owner."

From above us came Mr Hoo's warning. "Hoo. Hoo. Hoo."

My stomach tipped over. "Someone is coming."

"Do we think this is the Beast of Whittle Woods?" Finbarr whispered.

"Maybe." I stroked the reindeer's nose and it

made a peculiar coughing sound. "If it is, we can't let them find it." I started to think, rapidly trying out different scenarios. Send it back into the cave? Set it free? No to both of those. "We're going to have to take it back to the inn."

"We don't have a stable—"

"We'll think of something. Come on." Once more I tugged on the reindeer's harness and he obliged me by following without fuss. We walked together, not particularly quickly. Given how narrow the pathway through the trees was here, I found myself thwacked in the face repeatedly by bushes and branches as I tried to navigate a way through without the reindeer either treading on my toe or getting his antlers stuck in low level branches.

Above us Mr Hoo took off and circled above us. From some distance behind I could hear the search party thrashing their way through the forest.

"Keep going," I said, speeding up and taking risks where we hadn't before; neglecting to look where I could place my feet, trusting to providence that all would be okay, until finally I could see the ribbon of energy that marked the boundary of the inn. Finbarr came up to flank the reindeer's left-hand side and between us, each keeping a tight hold of the harness, we pushed through the perimeter, through the familiar resistance, and then popped out on the other side.

Now we were finally on home territory I wasn't too concerned about Talbot-Lloyd and his combative team of hunters. They wouldn't dare follow me on to my land. Nonetheless, I still walked as quickly as I could, as speedily as the terrain would allow, eager to put as much distance between them and us.

We skirted the marsh and walked on to the clearing in the centre of Speckled Wood. From there the paths were well trodden, wide and clear and I could breathe a little easier. We slowed down a little, and then, at last, I could make out the lights of the inn ahead of us. As we walked out onto the lawns, I released the tension in my shoulders.

"Let's take him to the large storage shed out the back," I suggested. "The one where we keep the big ride-on lawnmower. There's plenty of space in there."

"Right you are. That's a good idea. We could do with some straw though."

"We'll have to get some in the morning." I wondered where I could get some locally without arousing suspicion. Or would it matter? Rhona in Whittle Stores would know. "We'll make sure he's fed and watered tonight. That's the best we can do."

"I'll see to that. I'm good with horses."

"He's a reindeer," I reminded him.

"Well there is that. I'm good with them too."

I shot a look at Finbarr across the reindeer's back. I could just about make out his face. "You have experience of reindeer?"

"Loads." I pursed my lips, not believing him. "All of twenty-five minutes' worth," he admitted.

The reindeer emitted an odd breathy snickering sound.

"At least he thinks you're funny," I said with a smile.

"It's nice to be appreciated." Finbarr patted the reindeer's flank and it turned its head to look at him.

"It either likes you or it's going to kill you," I said. "Either way, that works for me. I'm sure Zephaniah would enjoy looking after him actually. He often talks about the horses they had here at the inn before The Great War."

"Well that would be right. The problem is, Zephaniah was taken sick this morning."

"Oh no! Was he?" I hadn't heard that.

"Aye. Your great-grandmother has whisked him away to the attic with all her other unfortunate victims."

I hid a smirk. "I'm sure she's doing her best."

"Ah, I know," Finbarr cooed, contrite. "To be sure she is."

"But alright, if Zephaniah isn't available, I guess you get to look after the reindeer after all."

"Will we start looking for his owner in the morning, are you thinking?"

"Yes. In fact, I may just have a quick Google tonight. Someone may have misplaced one locally. I'll also get Ned to bring you out some food for it. What do reindeer eat, do you reckon?"

"Carrots?" Finbarr guessed.

"I'll Google that too, just to be safe," I decided.

Mr Hoo swooped around, then flew down and landed on the reindeer's back.

"I think he wants a lift," said Finbarr.

"Hooo. Hooooo."

"Lazy little tyke," I said, and the reindeer snickered again.

"Herbs, ferns, mosses, grasses, shoots, fungi and leaves." I stared at my computer screen. I'd brought my laptop down to the cosy kitchen so that I could supervise some refreshments for myself as well as the reindeer. Charity had the kettle on and the biscuit tin open, and I was beginning to feel the blood return to my nether regions once more.

"I'm not sure the kitchen runs to that kind of thing," Charity laughed, joining me to read over my shoulder.

"We have mushrooms though, don't we?" I ran my finger over the word fungi. "Would that do?"

"Do you think he'd like them sautéed in garlic?"

I cringed. "Imagine garlicy reindeer breath. No. Not a good idea."

"I tell you what." Charity adopted a more serious tone. "Why don't we give him a bucket full of vegetable peelings, left over from this evening, and see how he does with that?"

Finbarr appeared at the back door, rubbing his hands together as he stepped into the warm. "That's a good idea."

"How is he?" I asked.

"Settling in nicely. He's a very even-tempered chap. He's had a little water."

"Better make it a big bucket of peelings," Charity said, reading over my shoulder. "It says here 'on average, an adult reindeer eats around nine to eighteen pounds or four to eight kilograms of vegetation a day'. That's a lot, isn't it?"

"I suppose if you were daft enough to only eat

vegetables and no cake, you'd need rather a lot of them to keep your energy up," I joked.

"Y'know, speaking of cake, Alf, I found some bits and bobs in the cave that I thought you might want to take a closer look at." Finbarr opened his coat and caught a number of items as they freed themselves, laying them out on the kitchen table. There were a couple of empty biscuit wrappers, and a few containers that had evidently once contained cake of some sort, along with an empty wrapper for a 500-gram bag of demerara sugar.

"It's rubbish," said Charity. "Well done on cleaning up the forest, Finbarr, but why would Alf care about the trash that someone has dumped in the forest. They need to learn to take it home themselves—"

I held my hand up to stop Charity in mid flow. "No. He's right. This is curious."

All that sweet stuff. It reminded me of Grizzle upstairs. "Or maybe not that curious."

"That's not all." Finbarr lifted up his jumper and retrieved a dark brown bag.

I took it off him. A woman's small leather backpack. One of the straps had been chewed.

"You found this in the cave?" I asked.

Finbarr nodded. "There were some odds and

ends scattered around that had spilled out. I stuffed them back in the bag."

I carefully opened the bag and peered inside, then drew the contents out. Mostly pieces of paper, envelopes. Sifting through them I realised they were letters addressed to Linda Cleary. "This must be the dead woman's missing bag. There was no purse?"

"This was all I found."

I held the bag in my hand. It still had a little weight to it. I took another look inside and located a small pocket. Slipping my fingers in, I made contact with something small and cold. I drew it out. A silver front door key on a bright red key fob bearing the legend, 'Keep Calm Linda'.

"Front door key maybe?" Charity said.

Finbarr nodded. "I reckon. If you like I could have a better look around the cave tomorrow, Alf. Maybe take a better torch or lamp with me."

"The police will want to see this," I said. "I'd better phone George again."

"You do that," said Charity. "I'll sort out supper for old Rudie Rudolph out there."

"Rudie? Is that what we're calling him?" I asked.

"It's very fitting," Finbarr smiled.

"He has a shiny nose?" Charity asked.

"A red one," I confirmed and pointed at my

computer screen where the information from reindeer was displayed. "Apparently a red nose is not an unusual occurrence in reindeer."

"Wait till you see it," Finbarr nodded at Charity. "It glows. Honest."

I put the phone down after speaking to George. He'd sounded tired. Unfortunately for him, the festive season was a busy time. When you forced families together in close confinement, and added alcohol to the mix, the results could be explosive. He'd had another serious case of GBH to add to his growing list of cases to investigate.

I had a feeling that Linda Creary was no longer his top priority, although he wouldn't articulate why over the phone. He'd also said he would send someone out to the inn to collect the bag and its contents and to scour the cave, but not until the morning.

I'd done all I could for now.

Still in the kitchen, I'd moved on from tea and biscuits to a glass of cherry brandy on ice. I twirled the glass in my hand, enjoying the tinkle of the ice cubes and the colour of the liquid. My thoughts skipped from George to Silvan and back again, really making no sense. I wished Silvan could be here, sprawled on the bench opposite me, teasing me about my cold hands or tangled hair.

But he wasn't.

Instead the letters lay next to me, most of them waterlogged and stained. I picked through them. The ink had smeared and smudged and to my eye were illegible; written with an ink pen, in an old-fashioned cursive with a slight slant to the right. I wondered who had been writing these letters to Linda. At a point in history when everyone seemed to communicate by email or text, writing letters seemed like a strangely antiquated thing to do.

Unless you were a vampire, but I didn't think that could be the situation here.

And why did Linda have the letters in her bag? She had otherwise been carrying very little. The only other contents of the bag were a packet of tissues, a ballpoint pen and some sugar-free boiled sweets. No purse or wallet, no credit card holder.

"I suppose it's not necessary to take your money when you go for a walk in the woods," I said out loud. "But then I'd expect to have found it upstairs in her bedroom."

Odd.

I retrieved one of the envelopes from the bottom of the pile and examined it. I could make out most of the address. London.

George had told me several of his colleagues had been to her place of residence and not found anything of any use, but now I found myself copying down the address myself. I'd known little about Linda, but if I could find out anything that helped to solve her mysterious death or could bring closure to her relatives, it would be worth a try.

Besides, I needed to go to London anyway. I'd find a way to fit in a little visit to Linda's address, somehow.

Silvan had always said I was nosy. Well he wasn't wrong.

Chapter Thirteen

"What do you mean you're going to London?" Gwyn asked me when I nipped up to the attic to tell her the news.

I stared around, appalled by the sight of so many sick ghosts. There were a dozen mattresses laid out on the floor up here, with one of my ghosts lying above each one. Luppitt and the other Devonshire Fellows (the brothers Waite sharing a bed) as well as Zephaniah and Florence and a couple of others, were all lying in bed, eyes closed, oddly quiet. The lamps were glowing in the eaves, and my great-grandmother had been pacing up and down taking temperatures and monitoring pulses, and probably, let's face it, not a lot else. Nothing that did any good, anyway.

"You're needed here," she added, her voice a little shrill. The ghost nearest us, an eighteenth-century fop by the name of Albert stirred and looked our way.

"Mother?" he asked.

"Mother?" I whispered to Gwyn. "Boy, I'm betting she's been dead a very long time."

"He's running a fever of at least 102," Gwyn said. "He's completely out of touch with reality." She looked a little worried. "I'm not sure I can help them."

"Well that's why I'm going to London," I reminded her.

"Mother?" Albert asked again.

"I wonder if I look like his mother," I mused.

"You don't look like anyone's mother, Alfhild," Gwyn responded sharply. "Tell me again what you hope to achieve by heading up to London."

"Perdita Pugh gave me the name of a doctor who might be able to help us. I've tried to find a way to communicate with him—Mr Hoo, carrier pigeon, letter—but apparently he only does it in person."

"You're required here," Gwyn said again, as though I needed reminding. We were now just a few days away from Yule and with Florence and Zephaniah out of action, that put more pressure on Charity, myself and Ned. I really needed to find some new members of staff.

"Mother?" called Albert.

I stepped forwards and leaned over him.

"Hey, Albert." I smiled down at him. "How are you feeling."

"Pale," came the response.

"You do look a little pale," I said, deliberately omitting to mention that as a ghost he always did. "You have the flu, but don't worry, we're going to make you well. You just need to lie there and rest. Can you do that for me?"

Albert nodded and closed his eyes once more.

Gwyn gave me a rather cryptic look. "Are you pretending to be that man's mother? He's older than you."

"As you said, he's well out of it. He won't remember."

"This is exactly why you should remain here. Besides your own duties you could be helping me out."

"I know," I replied, pulling a face. "I do fully appreciate that. But I have to go. These ghosts—our dear friends—will not get better unless I can find someone to help you." When Gwyn didn't reply I turned for the door. "Look. I'll leave on the early train, and I'll be back tomorrow evening. It's just one day. I promise."

"I think it's very irresponsible of you, Alfhild," Gwynn called after me.

Suddenly exhausted, my limbs heavy and my head aching, it was all I could do not to slam the door behind me. Instead, I tutted loudly and clumped down the wooden stairs.

I found Grizzle waiting for me on the landing. He cocked his head when I spotted him. He'd obviously been eavesdropping.

"Families, eh?" he said.

"I want a word with you." I narrowed my eyes at him.

"Oh that would be right." He folded his arms and knitted his eyebrows together. "Just have a go at the house guest because you're in a bad mood."

"I'm not in a bad—"

He pointed at the ceiling. "Having a little disagreement with your grandmother?" he asked. "I heard you. In fact, the whole inn heard you."

"She's my great-grandmother actually. Deceased. And you," I raised my voice, "and anyone else who happens to be listening in, should mind their own business." There were skittering sounds in the walls and I raised my eyebrows.

At Wonky Inn you're never alone.

"But you're going to London and you're

deserting the sick. I'm not sure that makes you a very nice person, Alfhild." He mimicked Gwyn's voice. It was uncanny.

"It's because I can't do anything for them that I'm taking the day away from the inn tomorrow." I began to march down the corridor away from him, before something pulled me up short. The conniving little weasel had almost made me forget that I had a bone to pick with him.

I whirled around.

He'd disappeared.

I considered chasing after him, but I was tired. I had an early start in the morning, so I needed to have a bath and set my alarm to ensure I work up on time.

My bed was calling me.

Grizzle could wait.

CHAPTER FOURTEEN

I'd long been of the opinion that it never simply rained in Tumble Town, it poured. Today proved the exception to that rule. As I walked down Cross Lane it began to snow. Thick flakes settled on my fringe and eyelashes, on my nose and upper lip. I licked off the ones I could reach, blinking rapidly to clear the ones from my eyes.

This was Tumble Town and I needed to keep my wits about me.

Tumble Town; home of the dark, the shady, the miserable, the mysterious, the wretched and those who needed to remain invisible. They all rubbed along together here in a series of narrow, centuries'-old, multi-storied tenements, located along winding alleys where the sun's rays rarely filtered. Grime lay thick on the windows, and while candles and gas lamps burned weakly beyond the glass, perhaps serving to illuminate the interiors, they provided little light for those pedestrians who dared to risk life, limb or wallet by venturing onto the seedy side of the town beyond Celestial Street.

Celestial Street lay behind me. There I'd find *The Half Moon Inn* where I'd often meet with Wizard Shadowmender for lunch, along with Penelope Quigwell's office and The Ministry of Witches. But for today—this lunchtime at least—I needed to take a little walk on the wild side.

As I passed *The Web and Flame* I craned my neck, looking up, searching for the approximate location where I remembered Marissa lived. I wondered if she'd heard from Silvan. As terrible as the temptation was to knock on her door and enquire, I had plenty of other business to attend to and a limited amount of time in which to carry it out. Reluctantly, I turned my head away and walked deeper into Tumble Town, along the alleys where the walls seemed to close in on each other, until you could barely make out a slither of the sky at all, and shadows lay everywhere.

I didn't have an address, just a name. Dr John Quicker. Perdita had suggested I look at the brass plaques that hung beside the doors of the houses down here. That was easier said than done. The plaques had been hanging for so long, centuries in some cases, that they were either encrusted with grime or had worn thin. I slowed my walk so that I could peer more closely at the legends posted here; *Witch at Arms*, boasted one sign, *Royal Potioner* said another, *Conjurer of Black Demons* claimed a third. I hurried by one that read *Cosmetic Alchemist*, squeezing myself close to the walls to allow other witches and wizard to pass me, their hats or cloak hoods pulled low, their faces turned discreetly away.

Nobody here wanted you to know their business and in return they paid no attention to yours.

Supposedly.

In reality, I now understood that any stranger's visit could be reported and gossiped about in the numerous inns and alehouses that littered Tumble Town. Some of the residents here patently couldn't help themselves because they were rogues through and through.

This was where Silvan originated from after all…

I stopped and lifted a gloved finger to wipe away the muck from a plaque of a particularly run-down house. The house could only have been a dozen feet across but stood at least four storeys. The wooden frames of the windows needed replacing, and the once white plaster on the front was grey with age and covered in green lichen where the rain had run down the side of the walls.

Dr Jonathan Quikke.

Jonathan Quikke? I pondered on the dubious spelling. I hadn't asked Perdita to spell the name and had assumed I had it correct; however, this was too close to ignore. I banged on the door with my knuckles. The sound was deadened by my thick wool gloves, so I pulled off the one on my right hand and tried again, rapping extra loud this time for good measure.

"Alright. Alright. I heard ya the first time," yelled an old woman's voice. On the other side of the door a series of locks were drawn back and I listened to a scraping noise as the handle was turned. It seemed to take an age, but at last the door opened, by all of about two inches. A pair of dark eyes above a sharp nose peered out at me.

"Yes?" Her voice creaked like a rusty gate.

I smiled my best smile, willing my numb cheeks to operate in spite of the cold. "Hi," I replied brightly. "I'm looking for... erm... John Quikke."

"John Quikke or his son Jonathan Quikke?" she barked at me.

That would explain some of the confusion about the name I supposed. "John Quikke."

"I dunno why I bothered askin' actually. It makes no blind bit o' difference which of 'em you want. They've both been dead for centuries." She started to close the door and I hastily jammed my hand against it.

"Oi! What ya playin' at?"

I removed my hand and tried to smile again. "I know he—John—is dead. He was recommended to me by Perdita Pugh."

"I don't know any Perdita from Adam." The woman scowled at me, decidedly unimpressed.

You don't know how lucky you are.

I took a deep breath. "And neither should you, Mrs ah—"

The woman shouldered the door open a little wider, then folded her arms and pressed her lips together. Why had I thought coming to Tumble Town would be a good idea?

"The thing is, look, I happen to know John Quikke is a ghost, and I'm in need of a ghost doctor."

The woman didn't say anything, just glared at me.

"I've come a long way," I tried. I wasn't above a bit of begging if it would get me what I needed. "I'm a ghost whisperer. I know he's here."

I wasn't above a bit of lying either.

The woman shook her head and was about to close the door again when a gruff voice from somewhere behind her called out to me. "It'll cost ya."

"I have money," I said. There was a long silence and then the woman stepped back, her place taken by an old male ghost, slightly hunched of back, hair long and grey and curly. He wore an old grandfather shirt and pair of long johns. Both might have been white or cream at some stage but now they were filthy. His skin, slightly translucent was sallow. His eyes, fortunately, burned with a canny intelligence.

Or cunning, I couldn't be entirely sure.

"My name is Alfhild Daemonne," I told him. "I am the proprietor of an inn in Devon."

"Not Whittle Inn?" John asked.

I nodded in surprise. "You've heard of it?"

"I think I even went there once. Used to venture down to Honiton for the Hot Pennies event. I remember the Daemonnes that ran it."

"Wow." I hadn't been expecting that. "Good memories, I hope."

"Oh yes. Yes." He nodded rapidly. "For the most part."

I decided to gloss over what part that might or might not be. I didn't want to open a can of worms. "I take it you were alive the last time you visited?"

"Yes. That's right. Would have been about 1838. Thereabouts. Nice place."

"I'm glad you liked it, because I need your help."

"As I said, it'll cost ya."

"No problem," I repeated.

He nodded thoughtfully. "And going all that way, well that's going to add to the cost."

Of course. "That's to be expected. We can factor that in by all means."

"Splendid." He flicked up a finger. "There's a charge for my cart too. And for Dobbin."

What did he mean by 'a charge for his cart'? "Dobbin?"

"My horse. He pulls the cart."

"Ah." That made sense. Or did it? "Dobbin is also... erm—"

"Deceased? Yes. And I'd like to say that I'm eternally grateful that he elected to remain in my service, but a more stubborn horse you never met. And what's more he eats his bodyweight in food every day, and his stabling costs me an arm and a leg. I'm afraid I'll have to ask you to contribute to that too, and to the stress involved in me actually hitching him to the cart."

"That's alright."

"Only, I have to hire a boy to help me with that, so it all adds to the outgoings, you know?"

"Yes." I could feel my bank account lightening rapidly as I stood in front of the miserable hovel. If I hadn't been so desperate for his help perhaps I might have spun on my heel and gone in search of Marissa for a chinwag instead and forgotten the whole sorry idea.

"He's an ornery so-and-so, but he does the job." Dr Quikke stopped talking for a moment and regarded me with what can only be described as calculated curiosity. His eyes shone, and his mouth pursed as he probably calculated how much he could sting me for.

I concealed my sarcasm as best I could. "Have we missed anything?"

"Supplies." Dr Quikke nodded.

"For Dobbin? I thought we'd taken care of those."

"No, for my own needs. To see me through the journey and during my tenure at Whittle Inn."

Tenure? "It will only be for a short time. I'm sure you would like to be home for Christmas."

Dr Quikke stroked his chin. "Ah. So you were wanting me to come down afore the festive season? Is that what you're sayin'?"

"Yes. As soon as possible." As soon as the words left my mouth, I knew what was coming.

He gave an exaggerated nod. "Well, see, that makes things a touch trickier. Coming afore Christmas makes it a rush job, so it does."

I kerbed my frustration. "Yes, but my ghosts are poorly now, and I'd like you to make them better as soon as possible."

"So, we'll 'factor' that in too, shall we?"

"Yes. No problem." I have no doubt a note of hysteria had edged into my voice. Just how much was all this going to cost me? I'd be bankrupt.

As if sensing my rising panic, Dr Quikke disappeared behind the door. I stood alone and shivered, glancing up and down the alley, sensing the eyes that scrutinised me from behind nearby windows, even if I couldn't actually see anyone.

When the old ghost returned he'd produced a notepad and a stubby pencil. He licked the end of the pencil and began to write down a list of things in odd curly handwriting. Beside each item he wrote a few numbers. Finally he totted the whole number column up and flipped the pad around to show me.

I screwed my forehead up and attempted to decipher his writing. "What is that? Twelve pounds, six what?" I gave up. "That doesn't sound like very much."

"Twelve guineas, six shillings and thruppence. The thruppence will be to pay for my tobacco."

"I have to pay for your tobacco?" I queried.

"It's medicinal."

I laughed. "It's very bad for you. You're a doctor, you should know that."

"I beg to differ, young lady. I recommend it for all manner of ailments and afflictions."

I groaned inwardly, wondering whether Perdita Pugh had purposefully sent me to the worst doctor she had knowledge of. Snow had settled on my shoulders and now the cold had seeped through the soles of my boots and travelled up my legs. I couldn't feel my thighs. Given that Dr Quikke was not going to invite me in, I decided it was time to take my leave and warm up somewhere, perhaps with the aid of a pie.

"So I can expect you... imminently?" I could only cross my fingers and wish Dobbin and the cart a swift journey.

"Indeed."

"Do you need the address? Just head for Whittlecombe, South of Exeter. You'll find me."

"I'm sure I will. Never you fear." He doffed an imaginary cap and with that he disappeared. I stared into the vacuum he'd left until the old woman came to the door.

"A'right then?" I could see her resemblance to the old man in her face. What would she be? His great, great, great, great granddaughter?

"Yes, thank you."

The woman handed over a sheet of paper. An invoice for Dr Quikke's services. Evidently she'd written out a physical copy I could take away with me. Her writing was slightly more legible than his. I noticed he'd added in a consultation fee for the time we'd been standing on the doorstep.

"Private enterprise, eh?" I grumbled.

The woman nodded. "Mind how you go," she said and closed the door.

"I will," I replied to the block of wood that now separated us. "Thank you."

Linda Creary lived in a surprisingly well-to do area of

South London. I'd known it years ago as a bit of a dump really, a rundown neighbourhood full of large Victorian houses divided into flats where the occupants had tended to be down on their luck or low paid wage slaves. Now whole streets had been gentrified and some houses returned to single owner occupier, with neat outdoor areas and huge shiny cars parked on the road.

Lynda had a small flat in a shared house. I double checked the address and gazed up at her window on the first floor; the key I'd found in her bag clutched in my hand. The blinds had been drawn. There was nothing to see. I stared at the front door, wondering if I would need another key to open this one. Why were all her keys were not on the same fob?

I pushed the door and it opened into a narrow hallway, one interior front door to my left, the stairs ahead. My stomach rippled with nerves. I shouldn't be poking my nose in Linda's business, but I felt I wanted to know more about her. I owed her that much. She'd been a guest at my inn.

Without looking around, and trying not to act suspiciously, even though what I was doing was by no means legal, I quickly climbed up the stairs. Only one front door here too. Evidently the house had one flat per floor. Number two. This was Linda's.

I fumbled with the key and finally managed to get it into the lock when, just my luck, one of the neighbours started to descend the staircase from the floor above. A small dark-haired woman, probably my own age, stared at me with an element of curiosity. She spotted the key in my hand and smiled.

"You're police?" she asked.

I tried to feign an officious looking façade and probably failed. "Kind of," I said, hopelessly.

"You have Linda's spare." She nodded at the key fob. *Keep Calm Linda*. "I used to look after her flat when she was away. She didn't ask me this time."

That would explain why there was only one key on the ring.

"You knew her well?" I asked.

The woman shook her head. "No. Not really. Just to exchange pleasantries, you know how it is? I collected her mail if she went away. Watered the plants. That kind of thing."

"But she didn't ask you this time?" But I figured if she had, she would have handed over the spare key.

The woman shook her head. "If she was only going somewhere for a weekend, she wouldn't bother. It was only when she was going abroad."

"Did she do that a lot?" I couldn't recall Linda having a tan.

"She'd take a nice holiday somewhere twice a year. She told me she had a bucket list, you know? Used to go all around the world. By herself. I was quite envious, but I don't think I could go alone."

Linda had no partner then.

"I suppose her family are going to sort out her estate soon," I said. "I'm just taking a quick inventory. For probate." I crossed my fingers and hoped my lie wouldn't rebound on me.

The woman shrugged. "Like I told your colleagues, I'm not aware of any family, and I never saw her with any friends. She went away to Thailand last Christmas and I asked her whether her family would mind not seeing her and she told me she'd been fostered as a kid, so had no-one to worry about."

I nodded as though I knew this.

"It's a sad business," I said.

The woman sighed. "Yes. She worked hard and she took her holidays and that was her life." She offered a wry smile. "Anyway, I'd best get on. Errands to run."

I watched her trot down the stairs, and once I'd

heard the front door close, turned the key in the lock and let myself into Linda's flat.

If a flat can smell cold, this one did. The building was old, and the heating had evidently been off since before Linda had headed down to Devon. I could also pick out the faint scent of decaying vegetables, but other than that and a slight mustiness, the flat seemed in good order. I knew the police had been here, but they hadn't left much mess, mainly because Linda had very few belongings. In the kitchen the work surfaces were clear. A small pile of towels had been stacked on top of the washer and dryer, and a single mug had been left upside down on the drainer. A cursory perusal of the cupboards showed me that Linda was organised but didn't cook a great deal.

The next room along the corridor was the bathroom. Again it had been left neat and tidy. The suite and tiles could have done with updating but apart from that nothing jumped out at me.

At the top of the hallway was the lounge. Fairly compact it housed a corner suite in light blue, with complementing cream and beige cushions. A glass table with a single coaster stood on a beige rug. A flat screen television adorned the wall and a couple of nondescript prints had been placed either side of it. However, Linda obviously loved the outdoors enough to want to bring some of it inside. There were numerous potted plants, a couple of Aloe Veras, a large rubber plant, some ferns and even a spider plant or two. Very seventies.

The master bedroom seemed immaculate although the police had evidently been in here and done their thing. I suppose I could have riffled through her clothes, but I decided that wouldn't tell me much, so instead I tried the final room. Little more than a box room, I could imagine that an estate agent would describe it as a second bedroom but to be fair, short of a crib, you were never going to get a bed in there.

Instead Linda had set it up as her home office with a desk, an office chair and a bookcase. She'd clearly had a laptop or computer of some kind because the printer and a pair of speakers remained in place, but the police had taken the main device away. The drawers of the desk contained an assortment of stationery but nothing else of interest. The corkboard above her desk had a couple of motivational quotes but no photos of any humans. A bookcase contained some fiction, and perhaps half a dozen books on marketing. I wondered if that's what she'd pursued as a career. Had she enjoyed it?

Nothing, with the exception of the plants, and

there were a few of those in this room too, gave me much of an insight into who she was or what she had been doing at Whittle Inn. I plopped myself into her chair, and spun it this way and that, thinking.

Given the restrictive size of the room, in order to spin right the way around I had to push the door closed. Hanging from a hook on the back of the door was a cotton shopping bag. It had a green design on the front along with the words 'Sunny Vale Garden Centre.' I jumped up and unhooked it, intending to take a cursory peek inside. I found a clutch of letters addressed to Linda, all using the same bland brand of commonplace stationery.

The police had surely found these, how could they have failed to? Had they dismissed them as unimportant? I poured them out onto the desk and sifted through them. There must have been a dozen, all written in the same hand. The postmarks told me the letters had been written over a ten-month period. Once I'd arranged them in date order, I could see the contents became fatter as time went on.

I opened the most recent one and drew out six pages, seeking the signature first. This was a letter from a man named Roy. I turned back to the front page and the address.

Bishop's Cottage

Rectory Lane
Whittlecombe
East Devon

Had Linda been visiting this Roy in Whittlecombe? Had she been fostering a love affair?

I plonked myself back down in the swivel chair and began to read.

Chapter Fifteen

I didn't need to enter the inn; I could hear the chaos that awaited me.

A cacophony of sneezes, coughs, moans and groans, throat clearing and sniffing. From every corner of the inn, from between the walls and floors, in the shadows, and the cupboards, the pantry and the storerooms. It sounded as though every ghost who shared the residence with me had succumbed to the flu.

I stood in the vestibule, inhaling the familiar scent of the inn and listening to the levels of noise. I winced to hear it. In the bar area, several of my guests were sporting noise cancelling headphones and I have to say that I had every sympathy with them.

I found Charity behind the bar, pouring free drinks for our guests in a concerted attempt to keep them cheerful, but the strain was beginning to tell on her face too.

"Hey boss," she said when she spotted me. "Thank heavens you're back."

"Where's Ned?" I dropped my bag under the counter out of the way.

She handed me a glass of the brandy she'd just poured and then decanted another for herself. "I'll give you one guess."

"Ned is poorly too?" I couldn't help but feel glum at the news. What would I do without Ned? He was the backbone of the inn, always available when I needed an extra pair of hands, forever level-headed and willing to undertake any task no matter how menial. Always even-tempered and quiet.

And a mean dancer to boot.

"They're all ill!" Charity drained her glass. "Even Monsieur Emietter. Do you know who cooked dinner tonight?"

I looked around, scared of what the answer might be.

Charity pointed at herself. "I did. Little old me."

"I didn't know you could cook. Wow." I tried to enthuse but it sounded more like a cry of dismay.

Charity snorted and poured another brandy, a

larger version of the one she'd just consumed. "That's because I can't."

I regarded her for a moment. "How was that then? The cooking experience?"

"Best you don't ask."

I nodded and raised my glass to her. We chinked them together and I drank my brandy down in one. "I'll sort something out for breakfast."

"Just as long as it isn't *you* cooking either, that will be fine."

I frowned. "Come on. I'm not that bad. Anyone can fry an egg."

Charity guffawed with genuine mirth. "You think? I've had one of your omelettes before if you recall." She shuddered. "Never again." She spotted Frau Krauss waving and winking at me, before making her way over to see what the German witch required.

The talk of food had my stomach grumbling. I hadn't managed anything more than a hasty and tired sandwich while waiting for my train home from Paddington. I wondered what Charity had ended up cooking in Monsieur Emietter's absence and whether any of it had been left. I figured I could concoct that old standard, cheese on toast, for myself if there was nothing else doing. I drifted down the back passage to the kitchen and stared in horror at the sight that awaited me.

I hadn't quite realised how much I relied on the Ghostly Inn Clean Up Crew until this precise moment.

Dishes, pans, baking sheets, mixing bowls, cutlery and utensils were piled high in the sink and along every inch of available work surface. There were pans of dried out food on top of the cooker. The huge oven had been left on and inside I could just about make out a couple of cremated fowls. Chopping boards and sharp knives lay on Monsieur Emietter's workstation, along with entrails and vegetable peelings. If the French chef could have seen this, he would have packed his bags and left Whittle Inn without so much as a by-your-leave—or whatever the French equivalent of that happened to be.

My mouth open in dismay, I moved across the floor to switch off the oven; my feet slithered on spilled food.

I'd never seen anything quite like it, not even on the day that I'd interviewed for the chef position over eighteen months previously. Had Charity really managed to create this much disorder on her own?

Impressive.

With only a few days to Yule and another couple to Christmas, the kitchen should have been smelling of cinnamon and orange, candied peel, sage stuffing, chocolate log and brandy snaps. Instead, I could imagine that the inside of an abattoir would be more fragrant than Whittle Inn's kitchen right now.

Just suppose the Food Standards Agency had decided to pay me a sneak visit today? I shuddered.

I couldn't deal with this chaos by myself, but without a Ghostly Inn Clean Up Crew, what was a witch to do? I'd be here until the wee hours cleaning up the mess even if I found an extra pair of hands.

I plucked my mobile from my pocket and lit up the screen. My heart skipped a little beat of happiness, a missed call from Silvan. I wanted to call him back instantly but knowing he wouldn't be able to come to my rescue, I decided to put that off. I couldn't imagine him getting all domestic in the kitchen anyhow. Instead I thumbed through my contacts until I found Millicent.

"Do you know any spells to restore a kitchen to a clean state?" I asked when she picked up.

I finished cleaning some time after two in the morning. After finally placing the mop and bucket back in the boiler room where it resided, I slunk along the hallway, every part of me weary, to join Charity in the bar. There were still four or five guests up, playing cards or snoozing in their chairs by the fire.

"Do me a favour," I said as I dumped myself down on a bar stool. "The next time Monsieur Emietter is indisposed, just send out for pizza for the whole inn, okay?"

"Deal," Charity smirked, and offered to pour me a drink. I shook my head. We needed to be up at six to start the breakfast service.

"Millicent is going to come and help me do breakfast," I told her, "so you concentrate on the waiting side."

"Will do, boss," Charity said. "I think I can manage that."

I glanced around the room, taking in the few witches gathered around tables, still drinking. "You know what? I know it's unprecedented, but I think we're going to close the bar tonight, otherwise neither of us are going to get any sleep at all." I nodded at my green-haired manager. "You go on up, I'll sort this."

I was prepared for protests from my guests, but they understood the situation. Clearing the bar actually took me less time than I'd imagined. I surveyed the collection of glasses and decided I'd had my fill of washing up for the night. I strolled around, switching the lights off everywhere, leaving only the ones in the vestibule and the one on the stairs illuminated, in order that my more nocturnally minded guests could find their way around when they came in from their overnight rambles.

I made a beeline for the back stairs when something occurred to me. The fire had almost died out. This would never happen on Florence's watch. She was fastidious about such things. The inn didn't have the same vibe without her presence. I smiled to think how she would have loved the opportunity to cook a whole dinner in Monsieur Emietter's absence.

I regarded my great-grandmother's portrait hanging in pride of place above the fire. Her eyes glowed brightly. I really ought to go up and let her know I'd returned home safe and sound. I could check to see whether her ministrations were making a difference too, but I found I didn't have any energy left. Instead I climbed up the stairs only as far as the next floor and slipped into my own bedroom. Mr Hoo, perched on the windowsill, turned his head around and hooted softly at me.

"I told you I wouldn't be gone long," I said. "Are you going out hunting tonight?"

"Hoooo."

"Yes," I agreed. "It is brass monkeys' weather. Mind how you go, or your wing tips will freeze up."

My mobile rang as I started to pull my robes off.

Silvan. I'd meant to return his call of course but hadn't yet had the chance.

"Hello." I smiled through my exhaustion. "Why are you calling now? I could have been asleep."

"I sensed you weren't. You've had a long day."

"Aren't they all?" I settled back on my bed. "But truth to tell, I've been in Tumble Town."

"What were you doing there?" I heard the surprise in his voice.

"It's a long story. I was looking for a doctor. One that Perdita Pugh recommended. We have stupid levels of sickness here. A complete contagious outbreak of ghost flu."

"A ghost doctor? That's a novelty. Did you find one?"

"I did."

"That's great. You can find anything you need in Tumble Town. You do have to be careful though."

"I was." I yawned. I couldn't help myself.

"You're tired." He sounded sympathetic. He also

sounded wide awake. I wondered where in the world he could be. Somewhere safe, I hoped. "I should leave you to it."

"I could do with forty winks," I admitted.

"I'll go then."

"Silvan?" I jumped in before he could put the phone down. "Will you make it here? For Christmas?"

"Aww, Alfie." His voice was a purr in my ear. "I doubt I can. I'm so tied up here. I'm sorry."

I thought of Linda, and how her neighbour had said she liked to escape for Christmas. A conscious choice she made, rather than spend it alone. "It's okay," I said.

But it really wasn't.

"I wanted to ask you if I could take a few days and go home to visit my family." Finbarr's filthy fingers fondly scratched the reindeer's neck. I'd brought him out a cup of tea and a fried egg sandwich—cooked by my own fair hands I might add. It looked alright.

Slightly taken aback I almost withdrew the hand containing the sandwich. "You're free to do what you want, you know that. I have no designs on keeping you here longer than you want to stay."

"Ah it's not like that, to be sure. I'd like to go home and see my old ma, that's all. But I can see how short staffed we are at the moment." Finbarr hurriedly took the plate and mug from me before I could change my mind about offering him breakfast.

I shoved my hands in my coat, to protect them against the icy bite in the air. I'd found him in the shed with the reindeer, but it wasn't much warmer in here than it was outside. At some stage yesterday Finbarr had built a temporary fence all the way around the shed which helped to keep the reindeer safe without locking him away.

I performed a mental head check of the inn's ghosts. The only ghosts I knew of that were still of sound mind and body were my great-grandmother, and a little boy I knew only as Pee Pee. Pee Pee liked to run around the house and the grounds shouting Pee Pee at the top of his voice. I had no idea what his story was because I'd never managed to get close enough to find out. Gwyn didn't know either. I'd sent word out via Vance in Speckled Wood, and Wizard Shadowmender via the orb, that if my father Erik Daemonne was anywhere in the vicinity I'd appreciate his assistance. But like Silvan, he was off doing his own wizarding thing—in my father's case fighting The Mori—and I could only expect him when I saw him.

I could hardly stop Finbarr from taking a couple of days' well-earned leave, could I? "You definitely should go." I told him. "We'll manage."

Somehow.

"I could ask Mr Kephisto to come out here and check on you. I'm sure he wouldn't mind."

"That would be great. Thank you." I acquiesced graciously, after all, I didn't consider myself to be in any position to act all heroically and turn down offers of help.

"What about old Rudie here?" I asked. "I've had no luck so far tracking down anyone that's lost a reindeer. Nothing on social media or in the papers."

"I was thinking to leave the pixie—"

"No."

"I'm sure the pixies—"

"Under no circumstances," I said firmly and fixed Finbarr with an evil eye. He lapsed into chuckles.

"Had you there for a moment, Alf."

"Ha ha," I pretend-sniggered, decidedly unamused.

Finbarr straightened his face and coughed. "Well what about your little faery pal?"

"Is that another jape?" I growled.

"Not at all. He was a great help yesterday. He has a way with animals. Especially this one."

Of course. I'd been meaning to have a chat with Grizzle about the cave and the reindeer. All those sweet wrappers and the sugar in the cave? Who could have been hanging out there but my sweet-toothed faery visitor? If the reindeer had also made the cave his temporary shelter then it stood to reason they knew each other already.

"And he was good with the children too." Finbarr took a bite of the sandwich I'd given him, and I watched as yellow yolk oozed out of the bread and onto his fingers.

"What children?"

Finbarr finished the first half of his sandwich in four bites and licked his fingers clean. "They came up from the village. Word has got around that we have a reindeer up here and he's proving to be a star attraction."

I rolled my eyes. "Honestly, no-one can keep anything secret in Whittlecombe."

"I'm sure there's no harm done. This close to Christmas all the kiddies want to see Father Christmas, but meeting his special reindeer is a treat in itself, I reckon."

Now that could be a money-spinning idea. "If you weren't heading back to Ireland we could dress you up as the great man himself."

Finbarr smiled. "I think Mr Kephisto would make a great lookalike for old Santy Claus and he wouldn't even need a fake beard."

"Very true."

"I expect we'll have some more kids up here today, so if the faery is happy to help me out again, I'd certainly appreciate it."

"Alright. I'll have a word," I agreed.

As I turned to go, Finbarr called me back. "What shall I do with these?" He held up a couple of letters addressed to Father Christmas at the North Pole.

"Did the children give you these?" I asked, and Finbarr grinned.

"Yes. They borrowed some paper and envelopes from Charity. A few of the other kids who saw them do it said they would be back today with their own letters."

"How sweet." I took the letters from him. "I'll drop them down at the post office later. I think Royal Mail sends them on somewhere. I might have to write one myself."

"What would you ask for?" Finbarr asked.

I screwed my face up. *Company*, I wanted to say, but what I actually said was, "Warmer gloves".

"I hear you have a reindeer on your land."

It being close to the last posting day before Christmas, the queues in the post office had grown to epic proportions. When I'd joined the back of the line I'd actually still been on Whittle Lane, that's how long it was. Once I was inside the small post office I could see why. There was only one person serving. I tutted and settled in for the long haul, reminding myself to keep a stock of stamps in my office in future and save myself the long wait.

Unfortunately, I hadn't reckoned on the company I'd be keeping. Gladstone Talbot-Lloyd had followed me into the post office and cut in line so that he could verbally assault me.

I glared up at him, struggling to hide my revulsion when he asked me about the reindeer. "Temporarily," I said, hoping he'd hear the insinuation that I knew exactly where the creature belonged, and he should keep his hands off.

"Is it our Beast do you think?"

I shook my head. How predictable of him. "I'd say definitely not. This reindeer is an absolute sweetheart and he would never attack anyone."

"Not even if it was cornered?" Talbot-Lloyd asked. "Wild creatures can be unpredictable, especially when they feel threatened."

I took a deep breath and met his sneering look with a cold one of my own. "Not this one. Firstly, he's tame and not wild, and secondly, Whittle Inn is the last place he'd feel threatened. We're treating him well."

"It's just I have to prioritize the safety of the residents of Whittlecombe, and if I thought the animal was a threat—"

"It isn't," I repeated, my voice firm.

Talbot-Lloyd shrugged. "Fair enough. So you don't need me to bring my rifle and sort the problem out for you?"

The palms of my hands itched. I longed to pluck a hex out of the air. For one wild moment I contemplated a spell that would melt Talbot-Lloyd down into a puddle of wax that I could shape candles from. I'd enjoy burning those for the rest of my days.

Instead I swivelled away from him, staring pointedly forwards; resisting the urge to turn back and slap him when he laughed at my rather obvious ire.

Eventually after another twenty-five excruciating minutes I made it to the counter and handed over the messages to Santa as well as a couple of business letters of my own, then I pushed past Talbot-Lloyd so that I could hot-foot it back outside into the freezing December air. Relieved to be free of the stultifying atmosphere inside, I sucked in a lungful of oxygen with evident relish.

"Better?" Mr Bramble, sitting on a wooden bench and waiting patiently for the queue to go down, chuckled.

"Much better," I laughed with him. "Brrr. It's certainly not getting any warmer, is it?"

"That sky is laden with snow." He poked his walking stick up at the thick milky-white cumulus above us.

"Do you reckon?" I didn't. I smiled down at Mr Bramble. He appeared increasingly frail to my eyes, and I worried about him. He was an older gentleman, but he had always been so fit and active until the events that had unfolded at the Psychic Fayre in April.

"I do." He winked at me. "You don't need to be a witch to read the weather, young Alf."

I laughed.

"Did you get your letters posted?" he asked me.

I'd shown him the letters I'd be posting to Father Christmas when I'd spotted him on the seat on my way inside earlier.

"I did." Thinking about letters reminded me of the ones from Roy to Linda Creary.

Mr Bramble had lived in the village his whole life. "Did you know Linda Creary?" I asked him. He looked surprised at the sudden change of subject.

"No." He shook his head. "She was the young woman found in the forest the other day, wasn't she?"

"That's right." I thought for a moment. "Not so young. Maybe you knew her by a different surname?"

"I didn't meet her, so I'm afraid I don't know whether I'd have recognised her."

"No." Why should he have? I tried a different tack. "What about someone named Roy? Lives at Bishop's Cottage on Rectory Lane."

Mr Bramble smiled. "Yes, yes, I know Roy. We were at school together. Well... I was in the same class as his brother. Roy's a few years younger. He's not been well for a long time. You never see him around the village anymore. He was a good cricketer back in the day though. Very sad. He lost his son, you know. In the Forces, he was. Then his wife left him.

But that was a long time ago too. He has to have carers in now to help him with his dinner and cleaning and stuff."

"What's his surname?" I asked.

"Lear. As in King Lear."

"Roy Lear," I repeated. "Do you think he would see me?"

"Yes I'm sure he would. By all means pop round. He's a friendly chap. I ought to go myself." He laughed. "You've made me feel guilty now, Alf."

"It's the time of year we all need to check on our neighbours," I said, thinking of Mara the Stormbringer living deep in the forest with only her faery changeling for company. I should make an effort to visit her too.

"That's so true. Pass on my regards to Roy, Alf, and tell him I'll come and see him before Christmas."

"I will do," I promised.

CHAPTER SIXTEEN

I intended to make visiting Roy a priority, but firstly I needed to ensure the few workers I still had at the inn were managing. Millicent had agreed to help us out for a couple of days, until hopefully either Florence or Monsieur Emietter were well again.

That was assuming ghost influenza wasn't as deadly as the 1918-1919 super virus, and they were both going to get well, of course.

I tried to think positively as I walked back up the drive to my wonky inn, and also to consider all options. Okay, I wasn't the world's greatest cook, but I could do things on toast for lunch, and in my younger days I had eaten—and therefore cooked—a great deal of pasta. Even now, the kitchen always had pasta available on the menu, although to be fair, Monsieur Emietter always prepared it from scratch. I couldn't stretch to that, but I knew Whittle Stores kept some decent dry stuff on their shelves. Add a tin of tomatoes and a few teaspoons of dried herbs *et voila*! Cordon bleu, Alf style.

But when your guests have checked in for the festivities and all you can offer them is student grub, you have a problem. I needed my ghosts to get well, and quickly.

Coming out from the shelter of the trees bowing over the drive, I rounded the corner and stopped and stared. On the lawn in front of the inn, in the exact place where *The Great Witchy Cake Off* marquee had once stood, was a cart. Not the kind of cart I'd imagined—flat bed and open to the elements—but much more like a Romany caravan with a proper roof. Nearby, a ghost Shire horse grazed on—I could only imagine given the heavy frost—ghost grass.

Dr Quikke had arrived.

That put a spring in my step. I dashed forwards, running onto the frozen grass, which crunched beneath my feet. Skidding to a stop, I could only admire the cart. Decorated with brightly coloured wording and illustrations, it looked like something straight out of a Victorian newspaper advert.

'*Remedies for all your ills!*' announced the largest legend on the side of the cart, painted in bright red.

'*Dr Quikke's Cigarettes for the Blessed Relief of Asthma*' claimed another. '*Chloride of Ammonia Inhaler to provide relief for Catarrhal Throat and Ear Affections, Loss of Voice and Bronchial Asthma*' said a third. '*Mineral Waters!*', '*Electric Corsets!*', '*Cocaine Toothache Drops!*' and underneath an impressive depiction of a woman with long flowing goddess-like hair, '*Dr Quikke's Hair Rigour Lotion to restore Length, Shine and Vitality!*'

Dr Quikke was no medical specialist. The good doctor was a quack.

"Why my dear, Lady Alfhild!" Dr Quikke parted a pair of red curtains and appeared on the steps of his cart. What a difference five guineas makes. He had donned a decent wool suit in a mix of dark plaids, a maroon silk cravat and an impressive top hat. He waved a silver tipped cane my way. "Can I interest you in my Snake Oil Liniment? Supplied directly to me by our sympathetic cousins across the pond? Or I have some '*Much Improved Arsenic Wafers*' that will clear the complexion and promote sleep that might suit you?"

Promote sleep? I pulled a face. Arsenic? Surely that would only promote eternal rest. "Er, no," I said, "Thanks very much." I hurriedly shook my head and slid a little closer to the front of the cart to get a better look at what he had inside. Shelves upon shelves of glass bottles and small cardboard boxes, decorated tins and paper-wrapped packages tied up with string.

"Dr Quikke—"

"What about ox-blood tablets?" He produced a large jar of red tablets, studied the label and then tossed them back. "Wait, no. You won't need those. They're to build up thin people."

I glared at him. "Dr Quikke!"

He gestured around at his goodies. "Cocoa? Chocolates? Both very good for relieving the effects of the moon. No? Condensed mince-meat?"

"Dr Quikke!" I roared. "Have you come down here on false pretences. You know exactly why I invited you here. I have an inn full of very sick ghosts. They have influenza. Your sole purpose—" I wagged one finger, "—that is, the single most important reason you are here at Whittle Inn, is to help me make my ghosts better."

"All in good time. All in good time." Dr Quikke produced a small brown bottle. "First things first. We need to do something about that agitation of yours. It's not good for the heart or the brain. I'm a true believer that most human afflictions start in the head." He pulled the cork out of the bottle. It made a satisfying popping sound. "What I have here are *'Effervescent Brain Salts. The Quintessential Method for Reducing Nervousness in Womankind'*."

"By all that's green!" I stamped my foot. "I am not agitated. Or nervous."

"You could have fooled me," Dr Quikke quipped.

I plucked my wand out of my pocket and levelled it at him. I would never have lashed out in anger of course, no matter how furious I was feeling, but the sight of it in my hand and poised ready to strike made for a useful threat. It stopped the doctor in his tracks.

"Very well, very well," he grumbled and returned the cork to the bottle.

"So what do you have?" I asked, stepping closer to the cart so that I could peer inside. "Anything that will cure influenza?"

"That's a thorny problem, isn't it?" Dr Quikke removed his top hat and tossed it deeper into the interior of the cart. I spotted a bunk bed inside, draped with red velvet curtains. It reminded me of my time at the Psychic Fayre. What a snug little caravan that had been.

"But one that's surmountable, I'm sure." I sounded more confident than I felt.

Dr Quikke scratched his head. "The thing is, ya see, there isn't an *actual* cure for influenza as far as I know."

I groaned. Of course. In his time there hadn't been. Come to think of it, in my time there still wasn't. How many times had I been forced to rely on fluids, rest and generic painkillers? Had I gone to Tumble Town on a wild goose chase? Was there no way to make my ghosts feel better?

"What painkillers do you have?" I asked him. "Anti-inflammatories?"

Dr Quikke rummaged on his shelves. "Deadly nightshade? Pure arsenic? That's a good one."

I whimpered, completely out of my depth when it came to the healing properties—or otherwise—of the herbs in abundant supply on Dr Quikke's wagon. I needed help.

"Stay here," I ordered him, not that he looked as though he was going anywhere. Dobbin munched contentedly on his ghost grass and paid no attention to me. "I have someone who can assist us."

Millicent wiped her hands on her apron as she

listened to me babbling on about Dr Quikke. "Please help me," I begged.

"But Alf," she gestured around at the trays of food she was preparing. Lamb chops with parsnips and carrots in a mint sauce gravy, chicken breasts with shallots and chunky quarters of braised cabbage, a spicy bean hot pot. On the stove, several large pans containing potatoes boiled merrily away, while a red wine and lamb stock reduced in a large frying pan. "I'm already helping."

"Oh you are, you are!" I grabbed her by her upper arms. "You're a goddess-send, you really truly are. But Dr Quikke is here with a wagon full of poisons and I don't want him ministering any of his quack remedies to my ghosts and killing them off once and for all. I need you to guide him."

Millicent stirred the pan of sauce. "Can it not wait twenty minutes or so?"

I danced on the spot. "It could I suppose, but I'm frightened he'll take off."

"Has he been paid?" Charity asked. She was sitting at the kitchen table with a cup of tea and her laptop, going through the reservations for the next few days.

"No, not yet. I'm going to have Penelope manage the transfer of his money from the inn's bank account because he wants to be paid in old money. Pre-decimalisation. By over a century."

"If he hasn't been paid yet, he won't go anywhere." Charity nodded, a knowing look in her eyes.

I slumped in place, misery radiating out of me. "Alright." I sniffed in disconsolation. "I just want my ghost friends well again."

Millicent laughed and shook her head. "Alf dear. What will I do with you?"

"Help me?" I asked in my most pitiful voice.

Millicent beckoned Charity over. "If you could just stir this for a few minutes until the sauce is smooth and thick and then turn it off for me." She pointed at the timer on the big oven. "When the buzzer goes off, the oven is hot enough for these trays. Put them all inside. Make sure the hot pot goes on the top shelf." She tapped the lid of one of the saucepans. "Keep an eye on these. Don't let the potatoes get too soft."

"Got it." Charity said and gave me a smug look.

"I owe you!" I blew her a kiss.

She smiled with evil intent. "Thank you. I'll have Christmas Day off."

"I don't owe you that much!" I said, although to be fair, I owed her far more. "Try not to burn the kitchen down," I shot over my shoulder as I exited the kitchen.

I waited while Millicent grabbed her coat, scarf and gloves and then led her through to the front of the inn. She paused on the steps to take in the sight of the cart with its glorious signwriting announcing its world-famous cure-alls.

"My goodness," she muttered, and followed me out onto the lawn.

"Dr Quikke?" I called, and he stuck his head out of the door. "This is my friend Millicent Ballicott. She's a witch, and a complete whizz at creating magickal potions. I'm hoping that between the two of you, you can come up with a way to create a medicinal potion that will be..." I glanced at the poster nearest me, "extremely efficacious in every way."

"But she's not dead," Dr Quikke protested.

"Quite right," Millicent replied. "Not yet a while."

"She doesn't need to be," I explained to him. "Millicent will tell you what you should put in the potion and how to mix it up, and you will use your skills," I made a leap of faith that he actually possessed some, "to create the finished product and then we'll try it out on a guinea pig."

"A guinea pig?" Dr Quikke looked bemused.

"She means a willing victim on temporary release from the hospital ward in the attic," Millicent told him and after a moment, although he still appeared a trifle confused, he nodded.

"What do we start with?" Dr Quikke asked. "I have foxglove? Hemlock?"

Millicent visibly shuddered. "My good man, we're trying to make people well here, not send them to the grave. We need things that nurture. That boost immunity." She poked her head inside the cart. "Vitamin C. Huge amounts of it is what we'll need to start with. Do you have any?"

"Vitamin C?"

Millicent sighed. "Yes. Do you have anything with a lot of lemon or orange?"

"Ooh!" Dr Quikke reacted with delight. "Orange peel?" He rummaged among his stores and produced a tin. "From Spain!"

"That's a great start. Now we need ginger?""

"Yes, I have plenty of that."

"And garlic." Millicent pointed to the strings hanging from a nail in the ceiling of the cart.

I relaxed. This might actually work.

"We should also be thinking about making a chicken broth," Millicent was saying. "The sooner we get that on the go the better."

"I don't have any chickens unfortunately," Dr Quikke said, his face dropping as he looked my way. "I didn't factor chickens—or butchery—into the bill."

"You don't have the wherewithal to make chicken soup? What kind of a doctor are you? It should be your stock in trade." Millicent tittered. "Get it? *Stock* in trade?"

I clamped my lips together to stop myself from laughing out loud.

Dr Quikke shook his head, obviously nonplussed.

"Never mind," said Millicent. "It doesn't matter anyway. Alf has ghost chickens out the back. You'll just have to kill and pluck a few." This oddity was true. In the wake of the filming of *The Great Witchy Cake Off* I'd ended up with both live chickens and ghost chickens taking up a corner of the grounds out the back. I swear the inn was increasingly becoming a smallholding.

Somewhere a smoke alarm began going off. Its incessant beeping suddenly wormed its way into my brain. I looked back at the inn with alarm. Charity had been left in charge of the kitchen. What had we been thinking? If she ruined supper, Millicent would not be impressed.

I took a few hurried steps towards the front door.

"Erm... Mills?" I called back. "You seem to have it all in hand. I'm going to leave you two to it. And... ah... check on Charity."

Millicent, otherwise engaged with instructing Dr Quikke on how to make chicken soup, waved me away.

Only Dobbin regarded me with interest as I scampered back inside my wonky inn.

Fortunately Charity hadn't burned the inn down, she'd simply set a piece of toast alight.

I grabbed the oven gloves and retrieved the grill pan from under the toaster, scrutinising the charred item in puzzled curiosity. "What, by all that's green, were you cooking here?"

Charity pulled a face. "A bizarre request from Gandalf. Toast smeared with set honey and sprinkled with sugar, which he wanted caramelised under the grill."

Caramelised doesn't usually mean burned, I thought, but bit my tongue. Maybe Charity and I both needed some cookery classes. Instead I grunted. "I'm telling you, that faery is on a one-way ticket to the diabetes clinic. I'll go up and see him."

"He went out the back. He's gone to see Rudie." Charity turned her attention back to the pots on the stove and started stirring things. "If you're following him out there, please can you take this tea he asked for?"

I collected the teacup and saucer from the side.

"And yes, if he asks, it does have nine sugars." Charity shuddered.

"Eww!" I grimaced and opened the back door to let myself out. "Back in a minute."

I'd wanted to interrogate Grizzle about what we'd found in the cave. For sure he'd been there with the reindeer. Who else would have eaten all those sweets and all that rubbish? I felt certain it had been him I'd seen in the woods that night, so he had to know more about Linda's death than he'd let on.

But any antipathy or annoyance I had towards the little faery dissipated as I approached the reindeer. I paused for a few seconds and watched as they stood nose to nose. Grizzle at less than half the size of the creature, nuzzled the reindeer's forehead, whispering soothing words to it. I smiled to see them, both apparently friendless, but happy in each other's company.

"Hey," I called, plodding through the grass towards them. "I brought you your tea."

Grizzle jumped and stepped away from Rudie.

"Sorry, I didn't mean to startle you," I said as I reached him. I noted his watery eyes. Had he been crying? "Are you alright?"

"Yes, yes, of course I am. I'm getting a cold." He sniffed hard. "Your wretched ghosts gave it to me."

I doubted that. They had the flu, not a cold, and given the way his mouth turned down at the sides, he definitely looked a little sad to me.

"Funnily enough, I have a doctor on the front lawn. I'm sure he could recommend something to kill a cold."

Grizzle growled at me. "I want nothing to do with your witchy quackery, thanks very much."

I suppressed a smile. He didn't know how aptly that description fitted the magickal medical practitioners in front of Whittle Inn. I handed over my cup and saucer. "It looks like you and Rudie are getting on like a house on fire."

Grizzle accepted the brew. After regarding the liquid suspiciously, he sniffed it a few times. "I hope it's sugared. The rainbow-haired witch in the kitchen seemed a little preoccupied."

"She's trying to keep an eye on dinner. But she's not a witch."

Grizzle snorted. "I'd have thought you knew your own kind."

I shook my head not wanting to get into an argument. "You like reindeer?"

"I love all animals," Grizzle said, and his voice became less belligerent. "I don't discriminate." He smiled at the reindeer fondly. "But yes. This boy is something special."

"Were you looking after him in the cave?" I pushed for information.

Grizzle shrugged and turned his face away so I couldn't study his expression. "I didn't see who killed that woman. I can't help you."

"But did you see anything else? Anything that can help the police?"

Grizzle turned back to me. "I don't think there was anyone else. Not before you. Just her. And then you."

"That makes no sense." I pursed my lips, a little annoyed with the faery for not being more cooperative.

"Sense or not, that's the way it was. Believe me, if I could turn back time, I would. I liked living alone in that little cave, away from the fortress and their busy, busy, meaningless routines and military nonsense. And then when this fellow showed up, I finally thought I had it all. Someone I could take care of, all to myself."

Now I understood why Grizzle appeared so upset. He'd found an existence that worked well for him and it had been taken away from him the moment whomever had killed Linda followed her to the clearing.

"You enjoyed the company," I repeated softly.

"And now you'll find out who he really belongs to and I'll have to let him go. Then what?" The bitterness had seeped back into Grizzle's voice now. "I can't go back to the cave. Hardly a secret now, is it? You or that nosy Irish witch will be visiting me every five minutes."

"Aww. That wouldn't be such a bad thing, would it?"

"I'd hate it!" Grizzle spat at me. I backed away from his vitriol, hurt by the turn the conversation had taken.

Grizzle's face flushed. "I'm sorry," he jumped in quickly, before I could turn to leave.

"It's okay." I shook my head. "I do understand that pull of needing to be alone and in familiar surroundings and yet still wanting company. We'll have to see what we can do to find you somewhere." I gestured at Rudie. "And maybe I won't find his owner. Given I've had no luck so far you might have to keep looking after him."

"Oh you will. Soon enough."

He seemed very certain.

From the distance came the sound of the smoke alarm again. I needed to head back to the kitchen. "That might be your lunch," I told the faery. "I need to go and check on Charity."

Grizzle nodded with indifference, so I retreated. Halfway back to the inn I turned around. Grizzle was sharing his tea with the reindeer.

I'm pretty certain Google hadn't suggested hot sweet tea made for nutritious reindeer food, but Rudie lapped it up.

Chapter Seventeen

Bishop's Cottage did not belong to Whittle Estate and so I had no prior knowledge of it or the tenant, save the fact I'd walked past it from time to time. Probably dating from the early twentieth century, and made from traditional red brick and a slate roof, I imagined it must once have been pretty. Certainly the garden—a small patch at the front that led around the side to the rear—had the air of something that had been well-tended until probably relatively recently. The front door had been painted post-box red but was now in need of freshening up. There was no doorbell, so I knocked.

I waited for some time, spotting movement through the dappled glass of the side window. Eventually a man with a walking frame and wearing a stained jumper unlocked the door and pulled it open, peering out at me through his thick spectacles.

"I'm so sorry to disturb you," I began. "Are you Roy Lear?"

His face changed and he gazed at me with eyes full of hope. "Linda?" he asked.

My insides crumpled in horror, and I shook my head. "I'm Alfhild Daemonne. From up at Whittle Inn."

"Oh." His face fell. "Yes, I'm Roy Lear."

"You were expecting a visit from Linda?" I asked. "Linda Creary?"

He perked up again. "Yes. Are you a friend of hers?"

How could this poor man live in this village and not be aware of what happened?

"Not exactly. She was staying with me." I faltered. It wasn't my place to break the bad news to him, was it? "What... How... Are you a friend of hers?" How much of a friend could he be if he didn't recognise her? He'd imagined I might be her. And yet, all those letters he had written to her.

"I'm her grandfather."

"Her grandfather?" I reeled with the news. Now suddenly everything made sense. The letters I'd read in Linda's flat in London, all from Roy, had told her about a man called Dave. I'd thought it odd. They described things Dave had gotten up to as a child.

Holidays he had enjoyed. There had been photos enclosed with some of the letters, depicting a gangly kid playing on beaches or riding a pony. A later photo showed him in the army cadets.

Roy had written to her often but hadn't know what Linda looked like. And he didn't know she was dead.

I stepped away from his door. "Can you excuse me for a moment? I really need to make a phone call."

Forty minutes later I'd made a pot of tea and we were sitting in Roy's living room with George and a family liaison officer named Lisa. I'd called George because it seemed wrong for me to proceed with giving the bad news to an old man with obvious health issues, and also because George had been at a seeming loss as to whom Linda's next of kin might be.

Well here we were.

For his part, Roy had taken the news relatively well. His rheumy eyes had watered for a while, and he'd accepted a tissue from Lisa, but he seemed more disappointed than anything else.

"I didn't really get to know her that well," Roy

was telling us. "She wasn't a great letter writer really. Didn't respond to most of mine. Just dropped me a line every now and again." He pulled half a dozen slim envelopes from beneath the books on his side table.

"You hadn't been in touch long?" George asked.

"About nine or ten months. She'd been doing some research into who her real parents were and got lucky when she managed to track down some details of my son. She found his birth certificate and that led her to me." He exhaled noisily. "Dave was born and brought up in this house."

"Dave was her father?" George confirmed.

"Yes. Yes. No doubt about that. Of course Dave's been dead for thirty-five years now, nearly thirty-six. She would only have been a few years old when he passed on, but in any case, he and Linda's mother were never together."

"Why was that?" I asked, curiosity getting the better of me even though I knew I wasn't supposed to be asking questions.

"Ah well, you see, Dave was in the army. He was based at Aldershot while he was doing his training and he fell in with this local lass, and she found herself in the family way. He did the right thing, asked her to marry him, but she wasn't too keen. As far as I know he intended to support her, but the split was acrimonious. She never really followed it up, didn't come to him for money. And then a few years later he died."

"How sad," I said.

He nodded, his eyes far away.

"Was he killed on active service?" George asked, his tone softening.

Roy offered a wry smile. "No. As it happens. He had a road accident while on leave in Gibraltar. The army were kind though. They brought him home. He's buried in the churchyard. He has a military headstone if you want to have a look." Roy seemed proud of that.

George nodded. "I'll certainly pay my respects to him," he said. He studied his notebook again and cleared his throat. "So, Linda didn't know anything about her father? Her mother hadn't told her anything?"

"I believe Linda's mother—and I'm ashamed to say I don't recall her name after all these years—died when Linda was about twelve or thirteen. Linda was fostered after that."

That much we knew.

"Then she just went on with her life... until finally she decided to try and track down any extended family she might have. That led her to me."

"But you hadn't met?" George asked and Roy shook his head. Tears welled up in his eyes again.

"And now we never shall." He blew his nose. "I did hear someone had died in the forest, but then Joanne who lives next door told me it was a Beast or Big Cat or something. She said there'd been a hunting party. I didn't put two and two together."

"No reason why you should have," George said. "I can assure you that it wasn't a Beast or a Big Cat that killed your granddaughter."

"Do you know who did?" the old man asked. "Have you caught them yet?"

"Well I kind of have some good news about that," George replied. He flicked back several pages of his notebook. "I attended the post-mortem a few days ago and we had full results yesterday. We're just waiting on tox screens right now, but don't expect anything significant from those." He glanced up at Roy. "Meaning she wasn't taking any medication and had no history of drug abuse."

Roy nodded. "I'm a big fan of those forensic programmes, young man. I know about tox screens." He gave a short wheezy laugh. "Besides, it sounded to me like she worked hard at her job and didn't have much else going on in her life."

"Apart from holidays," I said.

"That's right! Apart from her holidays." Roy pointed into his small kitchen and following the direction of his finger I noticed three or four of postcards on display on his fridge, held in place by magnets. "She sent me cards from the places she visited. That was nice of her."

"Sadly we think she suffered some sort of heart arrhythmia. The autopsy found evidence of heart disease and the thickening of her arteries. We think that she fell and hit her head while out walking."

"Heart arrhythmia?" Roy frowned.

"Like a heart attack," George said. "We're not entirely sure of the sequence of events. She had a skull fracture here," he indicated the left-hand side of his forehead, "but not significant enough to have killed her had she received treatment straight away." He sighed. "It was a cold night and the cause of death is being given as hypothermia with extenuating circumstances of heart disease and a fractured skull."

"You don't think anyone else was involved?" I asked in surprise. Grizzle had been right. There hadn't been anyone else in the forest with Linda that night.

George nodded. "That's correct. We are now treating this as an unfortunate accident."

"Oh no," I gasped, my hands over my mouth. "How terrible. If only I'd found her sooner."

Roy reached out to pat my hand. "Don't do that to yourself. The one thing I've found after all these years is that 'what-ifs' and 'if-onlys' will never bring your loved one back. What's done is done and we simply have to grieve in or own time and make the best of it."

"A wise old man," George said as I clicked my seatbelt into place next to him. He'd offered to give me a lift back to the inn. I'd have plenty of time to help Millicent with the final preparations for dinner, although to be honest, after my harrowing afternoon in Roy's company, I almost felt like throwing myself in a hot bath and weeping for a few hours with only Mr Hoo for company.

"I can hardly bear to leave him all alone there," I said, trying to hide my snuffles.

"You are an old softie, Alf." George inserted the

key in the ignition and smiled across at me. He looked exhausted himself. "Lisa will make certain he's alright."

I nodded. "Thanks for coming. I didn't think it was right for me to break the news."

"You did the right thing. And it helped to tie up a few loose ends." He stared at me with a certain suspicion. "How did you find out about Roy anyway?"

I grimaced. I hadn't come clean about my trip to Linda's flat in London, or to finding the letters. I shrugged. "It was something Mr Bramble said. You know Mr Bramble?"

"I do." George waited for more, but I pretended to fumble with a tissue and eventually he started the car and we drove along Rectory Lane looking for somewhere to turn. To our right the pretty church yard lay behind a low wall, some of the graves neglected, others carefully cultivated. We performed a U-turn at the Church gates and George paused to give another car the right of way. He glanced at the church yard now to the side of us, probably thinking of Dave Lear.

"So much death and destruction everywhere." George sighed, and I stared at him in surprise. It wasn't like George to complain.

"Are you alright?" I asked, concerned for his own mental wellbeing.

"Yes! Of course I am. Sorry." He checked his mirrors and indicated as he pulled out and we headed back down Rectory Lane, passing Roy's cottage on the right and eventually turning left at the T-junction to head back towards the village. He glanced at me to offer a reassuring half-smile with his eyebrows raised. "I'm just a bit done-in and I've too much work on."

"But you must be about ready to leave for your holiday," I said, not fooled for a moment by his forced cheerfulness. "Are you packed yet?" His face darkened but I continued on regardless. "By this stage of the approach to my holiday in the summer, I'd already packed and unpacked at least three times."

"We're not going," he said in a small voice.

"Maybe it's a girl thing?" I said, not sure I'd heard right. "Is Stacey doing all your packing for you?" I trailed off when he sighed and suddenly pulled the car over. He parked up and glowered at me.

"She's seeing someone else." He slouched in his seat. I gawped at him; uncertain I'd heard correctly. "There. I've said it. Does that make you happy?"

I struggled to process his words. "She's seeing someone else?"

"At work. One of my colleagues."

Boy. She really had a thing for policemen.

"George," I said softly, reaching out to pat his knee. "I'm so sorry."

"Yeah." George rubbed his tired eyes. "This bloke's girlfriend was at the station yesterday gunning for Stacey. That's how I found out."

I laughed in disbelief. I had a theory that people who insinuated themselves between other couples would often continue that pattern of behaviour in the future. "That's cruel." I felt his pain. "But believe me George, I take no pleasure in it."

George turned to face me properly. "I'm sorry." He exhaled slowly and rolled his shoulders back to try to relax the tension in his shoulders. "I know you don't. That was unkind of me. I apologise."

"Apology accepted."

He gave me a sharp nod, then released the handbrake. We pulled away from the kerb and headed up the lane towards Whittle Inn once more. "So to answer your question, I've cancelled most of my leave and the holiday. I won't get much of my money back but c'est le vie, I suppose."

We arrived on the drive. George stared curiously

as Dr Quikke's cart. A small fire had been built on the lawn and a large iron pot steamed above it. "What is that?"

"This is Dr Quikke. He's a quack. But with Millicent's assistance he's helping me cure the ghosts of their flu." Dobbin pricked his ears and ambled towards George's car, bobbing his head a few times and regarding us from the other side of the glass, his great jaws grinding methodically on ghost grass.

"Is this a ghost horse?" George swivelled his head to question me and turned back, open mouthed in fascination, to stare at Dobbin.

"Yes. It's Dobbin. He's an old-fashioned Shire horse."

"He's a stunner," George breathed, his face lighting up. "Wow."

"Dr Quikke swore blind he was a complete nutcase, a real problem, but he's as docile as the day is long." I shrugged, clueless as to why Dr Quikke had said such a thing.

"I have to hand it to you, Alf. A visit to Wonky Inn refreshes the parts other inns cannot reach." He tapped his heart and I laughed in delight.

"You're welcome here any time, DS Gilchrist. You know that."

George leaned over and we hugged, albeit a little

awkwardly given that he was still wearing his seatbelt and the gear stick was in our way.

"If you're at a loss for somewhere to be, come for Christmas dinner," I said. "I'd love to have you here."

"I'll think about it," he promised.

I opened the door and swung myself out, then smiled and leaned back in. "Don't just think about it, do it. Where else are you going to find witches, wizards, faeries, ghosts, ghost horses and Victorian medical men... and a reindeer?"

"You have a reindeer?"

"Now that would be telling. But if you come along on Christmas Day you'll find out, won't you?" I winked at him and slammed the door closed.

After a moment, he turned the car and returned the way he'd come. I watched him go, lifting my arm to wave until he was out of sight. Once he'd disappeared, my stomach twisted. I hated to think of him alone. I hated to think of anyone alone.

I recalled Roy's face when he'd answered the door and had imagined for just a moment that I was his granddaughter come to visit him.

Not for the first time that day my eyes pricked with tears. The world can be a cruel and lonely place sometimes.

Poor Roy.

Poor George.

Gravel crunched behind me and I turned about to see Millicent walking towards me wearing her apron and not her coat. Her face was pink, probably from the steam in the kitchen. She'd been hard at it, multi-tasking I expect.

"Is everything alright?" she enquired, evidently noting my red-rimmed eyes.

I nodded, feeling miserable but not wishing to burden anyone else with it. "How about you?"

"Excellent. I think we're making real progress. John is just boiling the ingredients up for the potion. We decided to add a little of his *Effervescent Brain Salts* and do you know, I think that will give us the pep we need. It should all be ready in about half an hour. In the meantime, we have the soup simmering on the fire."

A ghost iron pot on a ghost fire boiled gently with ghost chicken broth. I swear I could smell it though. My stomach rumbled.

"Will you help us persuade Gwyn to dose the ghosts up with our potion?" Millicent asked.

"Of course, although I doubt she'll need much persuasion. She's probably sick to the back teeth of that rabble of poorly spirits by now."

Millicent made a move towards Dr Quikke's cart.

"I'll give you a shout when it's ready. Where will you be?"

I glanced down the drive. George had disappeared on his way back to Exeter, but my sadness for his new situation lingered. Added to the empathy I had for Roy's loss; I must have made for one dour-looking witch.

"Are you sure you're alright, Alf?" Millicent asked.

I turned back to her. "Nobody should be alone at Christmas, should they?"

She shook her head, an emphatic no, while her eyes questioned me. That was enough for me. I didn't wait for a verbal response. "I'm going to head back into the village. And then I'll probably swing by Mara's too."

"But the dinner—"

"It's fine. I'll take Jed's van. I don't think I'll be long at all."

I ran inside the inn to locate the van keys. Just a few days ago I'd been lamenting the fact that I'd be alone for Christmas, but the solution had been in my grasp all along.

I had no need to be alone if I simply filled the inn to the rafters with other lonely souls. I had plenty of room. We could all bunk up together.

With a new sense of purpose, I perked up. I jumped into the van, slightly concerned whether it would start in the cold, but I whispered a little *start-first-time* spell and stroked the dashboard and within seconds the engine had roared into life.

I turned the heater up to full and switched on the radio, my heart full of enthusiasm for the mission ahead. As the van ambled down the drive I laughed and sang out loud:

Let's drink all the wine
And have the best time
Witching in a winter wonkyland

CHAPTER EIGHTEEN

We'd ended up delaying Yule until it had to merge with the Christmas festivities, but that didn't matter really. On the longest night of the year, I'd taken a candle encased in a glass lamp to protect it from the bitter breeze and made my way out to the clearing in Speckled Wood with just Mr Hoo for company. The Winter Solstice is a night for reflection and therefore at midnight I held my own ceremony. Wrapped in my thickest cloak, I knelt among the leaves for some time and gazed into the flame, remembering all that had come to pass this past twelve months.

The Psychic Fayre and my strange outing as Fabulous Fenella the Far-Sighted, thanks to the Cosmetic Alchemist, Cordelia Denby. That had been interesting.

My horrible dunking in Whittle Pond.

George's abduction. Both of those at the hands of The Mori.

The poisoning of Speckled Wood and the surrounding forest.

The small tussles with Talbot-Lloyd and other members of the community.

The big battle with The Mori.

The body in the wall of the inn.

Time travelling with Mr Wylie. That had almost been fun, but I'd never managed to conquer my travel sickness.

Then the producers of *The Great Witchy Cake Off* had brought the show to Whittle Inn and that should have been a sweet treat but had mostly been a sour surprise. Florence had become a superstar of sorts, and I'd overdosed on cake.

The vampires. How I hated the vampires. I could only hope to goodness that we would never hear from them again. The memory of scaling the walls of Castle Iuliad was still too fresh in my mind, and the terror I'd experienced was something I imagined would never fade away. Nightmares propelled me from my sleep regularly, and afterwards I would lie in the dark, gasping for breath, certain that death was imminent.

But, I scolded myself, *think of the good!*

I'd survived it all. I was stronger than ever both physically and mentally, and my magickal practice had improved exponentially, thanks in large part to Horace T. Silvanus.

Dark witch, mentor... and my love.

I watched the candle as it flickered and burned in front of me. Emotion bloomed in my heart, swelling until it expanded to fill my entire body. Even my skin tingled. I smiled in recognition. Silvan had lit a fire inside me that burned with quiet stoicism and kept me warm. I would never be alone if I held him in my heart.

After an hour of quiet meditation, I sensed that my soul had renewed. I let go of my sorrows and bid farewell to a year of darkness. Then I turned my face to the east and hailed a hearty hello to light and grace and a year of hope and magick.

What has been, is done. What will be, must be.

Late on Christmas afternoon, after I'd darted among my guests with yet another magnum of Champagne, and taken more orders for brandy, rum and whisky to be dispensed by the bar, I leaned against the fireplace for a moment to take stock.

As expected, I had an inn full of guests, but all my other available beds had been filled up with my friends. Rather than see Roy Lear alone over the holiday, I'd invited him to stay. He had now taken pride of place in one of the big over-stuffed armchairs closest to the fire. He held court with Mara the Stormbringer, who knew a thing or two about grief herself. Mara cradled the faery changeling Harys in her arms and chatted animatedly about the weather and her lonely cabin deep in the forest.

As long as she was happy, I was fine with that. Certainly Roy seemed in relatively good spirits.

Speaking of spirits, all of my ghosts were back in action. Some of them still looked a little peaky—peakier than normal anyway—but Millicent and Dr Quikke had happened upon a miracle cure and within forty-eight hours most of them were up and about once more. Florence and Monsieur Emietter had worked like whirlwinds in the kitchen, slaving over the hot ovens, in order to create a festive feast everyone could enjoy. The Devonshire Fellows were regaling us with cheerful songs—although the faintest hint of squashed goose squawking and I'd have fallen down on them like a tonne of bricks—and both Zephaniah and Ned were running the bar.

Colonel Archibald Peters and Dr Quikke were swapping stories of their travels. In Colonel Peters case I'm sure some of those related to Transylvania, but both were of a time markedly different to ours, and they compared notes, while drinking some odd-looking liquor Dr Quikke had found in his ghost cart.

I didn't ask any questions, but they certainly became merrier as the afternoon progressed.

Outside Dobbin and the reindeer appeared to have become bosom pals. I found it quite extraordinary that the reindeer, Rudie, could actually see and communicate with the horse. From the window, I'd watched as they put their noses together and harrumphed and snorted, stamping their hooves occasionally, their breath steaming in the cold. Grizzle had spent most of the day out there with them too. He'd groomed the reindeer and fed and watered him and now I could see him cavorting around, kicking an old leather soccer ball about, the reindeer and the ghost horse trundling around after him, whinnying and grunting in turn, their eyes shining with the fun of it all.

That was one way to exercise them, I guessed.

I'd given Charity the day off, because she more than deserved it, and instead I'd been doing most of the running around in her place. I didn't mind. It was my inn after all. Charity had elected to come to the inn for the day anyway, but she'd brought her Mum along. Mum had cosied up to Millicent, Jasper and Sunny, discussing—so I'd overheard—metaphysics of all things. I decided to avoid their company for a while until the conversation turned into something a little less mentally demanding.

Charity and George were sitting in the window, sipping champagne and playing dominoes. I stared at them now, heads down, happy in each other's company; the conversation casual and friendly.

That gave me a warm, fuzzy feeling.

Only Gwyn looked slightly out of place. She'd replaced her nurse's uniform with an elegant crushed velvet evening dress in Christmas green and a silver tiara, but she seemed like a fish out of water. I think she'd been enjoying the nursing and having something positive to do.

"Are you alright, Grandmama?" I sidled up to her.

"Of course I am. Why wouldn't I be?" She wrinkled her nose as though I were a bad smell.

"You look a little out of sorts," I replied. "Frau Krause is in The Snug looking for a partner for Bridge. Why don't you join her and—"

"Really, Alfhild, there's no need to fuss." She rubbed her forehead. "Perhaps a little later."

I backed off. "Alright. It's nearly time to light the fire anyway."

I left her to it, and alerted Ned and Zephaniah to the swiftly encroaching dusk. We intended to set Ned's bonfire ablaze as the sun began to set, and that time was upon us. Ned nodded and headed outside while Zephaniah began to fill glasses with the finest brandy and place them onto trays that we could carry outside.

I gathered up everyone who wanted to join us and led them through the vestibule and onto the lawn, Mara and Roy leaning heavily on their respective walking aids, Millicent ushering them along. We stood in a circle around the bonfire, while Ned tried to set it aflame and Florence handed around glasses of brandy. Finbarr tethered the reindeer with Grizzle's help, so that he wouldn't become alarmed by the ensuing festivities and the burning of the bonfire, while the rest of us tittered and shivered together, as each of Ned's attempts to spark a light from a match failed.

At last we had some success. Ned managed to create a spark and with the aid of a firelighter, the dry straw we'd added to the bottom of the stack of wood caught. With a whoosh, the twigs were suddenly alight, and soon the larger branches were gobbling flames in a frenzy.

Several of the guests cheered and the Devonshire Fellows launched into *Good King Wenceslas*. We sang along, while Ned and his lovely young milkmaid partner performed a graceful little dance that seemed to involve a lot of complicated hopping and looping around each other.

Eventually I raised my glass. "Everyone?" I called above the lute, the drum and the Crumhorn, and for now the music fell silent.

"Speech!" called Millicent, and Charity groaned.

"I don't want to say very much. We can go back to the business of making merry very soon!"

There was a swell of appreciation at that.

I smiled and continued. "It's been a trying year for me in many ways, but it's ending beautifully. I just wanted to thank you all joining me today and making this a smashing Christmas. You all being here—my friends and guests who have become friends—celebrating the festivities in my wonky inn, has made this one of the best Christmases I've ever had. Here's to us. Let's raise a toast. Merry Christmas!"

"Merry Christmas" echoed back at me, from all over the grounds it seemed. People slurped their brandy, glad of the extra warmth.

"And to absent friends," called Roy, and once again we all lifted our glasses in a salute to those who who'd come before and left ahead of us, or those still with us, but not physically present.

"To absent friends," I repeated quietly.

I sipped my drink and stared into the bright flames. Ned had done well, collecting all the dead wood from the grounds. It would burn merrily for a few hours, a beacon of warmth.

From behind me came the sound of bells. For a moment I assumed it originated from the Devonshire Fellows and I waited for them to start up with another Christmas song, but the shaking of the bells, while rhythmic went on for slightly too long. Charity walked towards me, her mouth open in surprise. I turned about when I realised that she, and a few other guests were not staring at me, but something *behind* me.

"Is that who I think it is?" Charity asked, her voice rising in awe.

I gaped in astonishment. Surely it couldn't be?

Gliding out of the sky came a sleigh the size of a railway carriage, pulled through the air by eight reindeer. A man with a big snowy beard and impressive moustache sat comfortably on the front bench seat.

With my back to the warm fire, I watched as the sleigh turned in a neat circle. As one, the team of reindeer lifted their heads and gently placed their hooves to the ground, landing effortlessly on the lawn in front of us and sliding to a neat stop. Now I could really appreciate the size of the sleigh. This late in the day it was devoid of presents, but my friends and guests and I could all have piled into the back of the sleigh and there would still have been room for every other inhabitant of Whittlecombe village.

Rudie grunted in excitement and pulled on his tether, intent on rushing to his friends. Grizzle clasped one hand to his mouth, his eyes filling with tears, and held tightly to Rudie's reins; tight enough that I thought he would never let the animal go. As Finbarr stepped forward to gently untether our reindeer from Grizzle's grasp, the old man in the sleigh rose. He leaned forward and with a virtually imperceptible wiggle of his fingers, the rope attached to Rudie's harness slipped free and Rudie bolted towards him.

Grizzle took a step or two after him, his arms held out, then stopped, visibly deflating.

"Whoa boy!" The old man laughed as the reindeer cavorted with glee in front of the sleigh and snorted, nose to nose with the front pair of reindeer who eyed him with delight and shook their heads. With another flick of his fingers, the old man had Rudie take his place at the very front of the herd. His leather harness flapped in the air and then entangled itself with those of the reindeer behind him.

Grizzle's head dropped, and Rudie, sensing his friend's sadness, lifted his nose and coughed and snorted. The old man in the sleigh listened with his head cocked, then turned and beckoned Grizzle.

The faery trembled at the summons and would have darted away, but Finbarr took his arm and propelled him forwards, whereupon the faery fell to his knees and lifted his hands in supplication. "I didn't steal him," I heard him tell the old man. "I promise. I was only looking after him. He told me he'd gotten lost. Took a wrong turning. He ended up in the forest and I just... I just wanted a friend."

The old man peered down at the faery, his red cheeks burning, and then he threw his head back and laughed. A great booming chuckle. "Ho ho ho!"

Startled, Grizzle stared up at the old man who

towered above him from his seat in the sleigh. "You're not angry?" he asked.

"Of course I'm not, Cleon Philbert Grizzle! You've done an outstanding job of looking after my reindeer. He tells me he's mighty fond of you. In fact... ho ho ho!... I'd like to ask you to join me at the North Pole. I could do with another reindeer handler."

Grizzle's lower lip trembled. "Me? You want me—"

"I only want the best. Are you the best?"

"Well I... I don't know."

"He is!" Finbarr volunteered, and I nodded enthusiastically.

"What do you say?" Santa asked. "Would you like to come along with us?"

Grizzle clamped both fists to his mouth in excitement. "Would I ever!"

"Ho ho ho!" The old man rocked with hilarity. "Then jump aboard and wrap yourself up well. We've a long, cold journey ahead of us."

I grinned as Grizzle leapt to his feet and with one excited wave at Rudie, clambered aboard the sleigh. He plopped himself down next to the old man and dragged a large furry blanket from the floor to curl up in. By the time he'd sorted himself out, I could just about make out his nose from within the cocoon.

The reindeers stretched and quivered with excitement, bells ringing at random, and then without further ado, Rudie jumped into the air, the others right behind him. The enormous sleigh lurched and became airborne too. We ducked as it flew over our heads, too close for comfort, wafting my fringe, and only narrowly missing the bonfire.

I spun about, watching as the sleigh doubled back towards us, a little higher now. The bearded figure saluted Finbarr and nodded at me. I thought he might have been mouthing a thank you, but above the crackling blaze of the fire, I couldn't hear him. Grizzle waved once before tucking his arm back inside the warmth of his blanket.

Passing above the large oak trees at the end of the drive, the old man lifted his arm and dropped something the size of a football over the side. I watched the gaily coloured box spinning as it fell to earth and disappeared into the undergrowth. Then the sleigh dashed away, at lightning speed, the runners leaving a trail of sparks that shimmered and burned and dissipated. Those of us left in its wake stared after it in disbelief.

"Did that really happen?" Charity asked.

Finbarr stood beside me and lifted his hand to wave. "Ah. To be sure I'll miss the little fella."

I assumed he meant Rudie. Personally, I would miss the grumpy little faery. For someone who had claimed not to like Christmas he had done alright for himself.

Nearby, Dobbin neighed a sad farewell. Dr Quikke moved over to make a fuss of him. "Ah what's wrong with ya?" Quikke asked the giant horse, who whinnied in disconsolation. "You're such a troublemaker, I despair."

I still hadn't seen a great deal of evidence of Dobbin's challenging behaviour. "I think he'll miss Rudie," I told Dr Quikke. "Maybe you should find him a friend."

Dr Quikke turned his nose up at that suggestion. "Do you not think one horse is enough for me to cope with? And so expensive. I'm not made of money."

"Perhaps a donkey?" Finbarr suggested, smiling at the giant Shire horse as Dr Quikke made horrified noises. "You'd love a little donkey friend, wouldn't you Dobbin?"

"Poor Dobbin already has a friend who's an ass," I mumbled under my breath as Millicent appeared at my elbow.

"You know, Alf, I'm thinking that parcel rightly belongs to you." I followed the direction of her gaze towards the trees at the end of the drive. "It's your land after all."

"I'll investigate." Curious to find out what we'd been gifted, and anxious to get away from Dr Quikke, I set off. I nodded at Luppitt as I moved past the merry musicians. "Please play something," I said. "Let's keep the party going."

I'd almost reached the drive when the opening bars of *Santa Claus is Coming to Town* drifted towards me. If you've never heard Bruce Springsteen on Crumhorn and lute, I suggest you haven't actually lived.

I couldn't be sure where the box had landed, so I had to search. I peered into the dark shadows at the foot of the first oak tree. The daylight had virtually faded now, and the light of the bonfire, while casting a glow in the sky, didn't reach the treeline.

Nothing to see.

I moved to the second one and this time I caught a glimpse of something gold. That had to be it.

But as I moved towards it, it moved; grew taller.

I should have been afraid—memories of the shimmering globes of The Mori were never far away

—but something about the warm energy this particular package emitted caused any brewing fear to evaporate. Instead of rushing for cover, I stepped towards it; inquisitive to see what it would be.

It elongated. Filled out. Became a figure.

A figure in a black cloak and a tall black hat. With dark shining eyes, and a smirk.

My breath caught in my throat.

"Silvan?"

"Who else?" he asked and held his arms open. I threw myself forwards, nearly knocking him over. "Steady, Alfhild. I've come a long way." He smelled of somewhere exotic, of sand and warm winds, dusky flowers and… yak urine.

"But…" I stepped back and stared at the sky through the skeletal canopy above us. The sleigh and its occupants were long gone. "How?"

"I hitched a ride from an old friend." Silvan pulled me close again and buried his face in my hair. "Dang, Alfie. I've missed you."

I squeezed him tight, my heart beating hard with excitement. "I've missed you too. I was afraid—"

"You need never be afraid." His standard response.

"—that you wouldn't come," I finished.

"I honestly didn't think I'd make it, but I wanted to be here."

"Everyone will be so pleased!" Taking his arm, I dragged him back towards the bonfire. As if on cue, Ned and Zephaniah started to let off fireworks.

Silvan and I stood at the edge of the lawn, arms wrapped tightly around each other and watched as the very stars began to explode in the sky above us. My wonky inn, lit from within, provided the perfect backdrop to this most glorious of holidays.

Over by the bonfire my great-grandmother, eyes streaming, sneezed and coughed along to the music. The last of the ghosts to go down with ghost influenza, she stood tall, a warrior to the last. Silvan and I watched as Dr Quikke sidled up to her, a glass potion vessel in hand, his top hat cocked at a jaunty angle. Gwyn batted him away, but with Millicent nodding enthusiastically, he persisted until he'd persuaded her to swig a draught from the neck of the bottle.

"What a homecoming." Silvan grinned and squeezed me to him, tight.

I pulled away a little and smiled up into his mischievous eyes. "You're the greatest gift I could ever wish for."

"I know," he replied, entirely deadpan, but then his face cracked, and that familiar grin appeared. "Merry Christmas, my love."

"Oh it is now." I beamed and reached up to pull his head to mine.

INTRODUCING
SPELLBOUND HOUND MAGIC AND MYSTERY BOOKS

Ain't Nothing but a Pound Dog

Toby dog suddenly has plenty to say for himself. The only witness to the brutal murder of his owner, Toby is hexed by a woman with evil intentions. "Speak to none but me," she tells him.

Wretched and misunderstood, he's incarcerated in the local pound. With a death sentence hanging over his head, Toby has almost given up hope.

But then he meets Clarissa. Not only is she a witch, she's a local investigative journalist, and—amazingly—she can understand what he says too.

Finally, he's found somebody who believes his story.

INTRODUCING SPELLBOUND HOUND MAGIC AND MYSTE...

Can Clarissa save Toby? Will they identify who killed his owner and why?

And will Toby ever eat his fill of sammiches?

Find out in the first instalment of this brand new paranormal cozy dog mystery series from the bestselling author of the beloved Wonky Inn books.

Pre-order Ain't Nothing but a Pound Dog now!

On sale 26th December 2019

Demand More Wonky!

If you have enjoyed reading *Witching in a Wonky Winterland*, please consider leaving a review.

Plans are on hold for further Wonky stories, so please let me know if you want any more!

Reviews help to spread the word about my writing, which takes me a step closer to my dream of writing full time.

If you are kind enough to leave a review, you could also consider joining my Author Street Team on Facebook – Jeannie Wycherley's Fiendish Street Team. As it is a closed group you will need to let me know you left a review when you apply.

You can find my fiendish team at

DEMAND MORE WONKY!

www.facebook.com/
groups/JeannieWycherleysFiends

You'll have the chance to Beta read and get your hands-on advanced review eBook copies from time to time. I also appreciate your input when I need some help with covers, blurbs etc. We have a giggle.

Or sign up for my newsletter
eepurl.com/cN3Q6L
to keep up to date with what I'm doing next!

THE WONKY STORY BEGINS...

The Wonkiest Witch: Wonky Inn Book 1

Alfhild Daemonne has inherited an inn.

And a dead body.

Estranged from her witch mother, and having committed to little in her thirty years, Alf surprises herself when she decides to start a new life.

She heads deep into the English countryside intent on making a success of the once popular inn. However, discovering the murder throws her a curve ball. Especially when she suspects dark magick.

Additionally, a less than warm welcome from several locals, persuades her that a variety of folk – of both

THE WONKY STORY BEGINS...

the mortal and magickal persuasions – have it in for her.

The dilapidated inn presents a huge challenge for Alf. Uncertain who to trust, she considers calling time on the venture.

Should she pack her bags and head back to London?

Don't be daft.

Alf's magickal powers may be as wonky as the inn, but she's dead set on finding the murderer.

Once a witch always a witch, and this one is fighting back.

A clean and cozy witch mystery.

Take the opportunity to immerse yourself in this fantastic new witch mystery series, from the author of the award-winning novel, ***Crone***.

Grab Book 1 of the Wonky Inn series, ***The Wonkiest Witch,*** on Amazon now.

The Wonky Inn Series

The Wonkiest Witch: Wonky Inn Book 1
The Ghosts of Wonky Inn: Wonky Inn Book 2
Weird Wedding at Wonky Inn: Wonky Inn Book 3
The Witch Who Killed Christmas: Wonky Inn Christmas Special
Fearful Fortunes and Terrible Tarot: Wonky Inn Book 4
The Mystery of the Marsh Malaise: Wonky Inn Book 5
The Mysterious Mr Wylie: Wonky Inn Book 6
The Great Witchy Cake Off: Wonky Inn Book 7
Vengeful Vampire at Wonky Inn: Wonky Inn Book 8
Witching in a Winter Wonkyland: A Wonky Inn Christmas Cozy Special

PLEASE CONSIDER LEAVING A REVIEW?

If you have enjoyed reading *Witching in a Winter Wonkyland*, please consider leaving me a review.

Reviews help to spread the word about my writing, which takes me a step closer to my dream of writing full time.

If you are kind enough to leave a review, you could also consider joining my Author Street Team on Facebook – Jeannie Wycherley's Fiendish Street Team. As it is a closed group you will need to let me know you left a review when you apply.

You can find my fiendish team at

PLEASE CONSIDER LEAVING A REVIEW?

www.facebook.com/ groups/JeannieWycherleysFiends

You'll have the chance to Beta read and get your hands-on advanced review eBook copies from time to time. I also appreciate your input when I need some help with covers, blurbs etc. We have a giggle.

Or sign up for my newsletter eepurl.com/cN3Q6L to keep up to date with what I'm doing next!

ALSO BY

Midnight Garden: The Extra Ordinary World Novella Series Book 1

Beyond the Veil

Crone

A Concerto for the Dead and Dying

Deadly Encounters: A collection of short stories

Keepers of the Flame: A love story

Non-Fiction

Losing my best Friend: Thoughtful support for those affected by dog bereavement or pet loss

Follow Jeannie Wycherley

Find out more at on the website www.jeanniewycherley.co.uk

You can tweet Jeannie

twitter.com/Thecushionlady

Or visit her on Facebook for her fiction www.facebook.com/jeanniewycherley

Sign up for Jeannie's newsletter

eepurl.com/cN3Q6L

More Dark Fantasy from Jeannie Wycherley

Crone

A twisted tale of murder, magic and salvation.

Heather Keynes' teenage son died in a tragic car accident. Or so she thinks.

However, deep in the countryside, an ancient evil has awoken ... intent on hunting local residents.

No-one is safe.

When Heather takes a closer look at a series of coincidental deaths, she is drawn reluctantly into the company of an odd group of elderly Guardians. Who are they, and what is their connection to the Great Oak?

Why do they believe only Heather can put an end to centuries of horror?

Most important of all, who is the mysterious old woman in the forest and what is it that feeds her anger?

When Heather determines the true cause of her son's death, she is hell-bent on vengeance. Determined to halt the march of the Crone once and for all, hatred becomes Heather's ultimate weapon and furies collide to devastating effect.

Crone – winner of a *Chill with a Book Readers' Award* (February 2018) and an *Indie B.R.A.G Medallion* (November 2017).

Praise for *Crone*

'A real page turner, hard to put down.'

'Stunningly atmospheric! Gothic & timeless set in the beautifully described Devon landscape .... Twists and turns, nothing predictable or disappointing.'

– Amazon reviewer

'Atmospheric, enthralling story-telling, and engaging characters'

– Amazon Reviewer

'Full of creepy, witchy goodness'

– The Grim Reader

'Wycherley has a talent for storytelling and a penchant for the macabre'

– Jaci Miller

Beyond the Veil

Upset the dead at your peril... Because the keepers of souls are not particularly forgiving.

Death is not the end. Although Detective Adam Chapple has always assumed it is.

When his ex-wife is killed, the boundaries between life and death, fantasy and reality, and truth and lies begin to dissolve. Adam's main suspect for the murder, insists that she's actually his star witness.

She claims she met the killer once before.

When she died.

As part of his investigation, Adam seeks out the help of self-proclaimed witch, Cassia Veysie who insists she can communicate with the dead. However, the situation rapidly deteriorates when a bungled séance rips open a gateway to a sinister world beyond the veil, and unquiet spirits are unleashed into the world.

Can Cassia and Adam find a way to shore up the breach in the veil and keep the demons at bay?

With time running out and a murderer on the loose, the nightmare is only just beginning ...

Praise for Beyond the Veil

'A 5-star winner from Queen of the Night Terrors'

– Amazon reviewer.

'Really got my heart pounding'

– Amazon reviewer.

'A nerve racking, nail-biting, spine tingling, sweat producing, thrilling storyline that keeps you on a razor's edge the entire tale'

– ARC reviewer.

'Female Stephen King!'

– Amazon reviewer.

MORE DARK FANTASY FROM
JEANNIE WYCHERLEY

Crone

A twisted tale of murder, magic and salvation.

Heather Keynes' teenage son died in a tragic car accident.

Or so she thinks.

However, deep in the countryside, an ancient evil has awoken ... intent on hunting local residents.

No-one is safe.

When Heather takes a closer look at a series of coincidental deaths, she is drawn reluctantly into the company of an odd group of elderly Guardians. Who are they, and what is their connection to the Great Oak?

Why do they believe only Heather can put an end to centuries of horror?

Most important of all, who is the mysterious old woman in the forest and what is it that feeds her anger?

When Heather determines the true cause of her son's death, she is hell-bent on vengeance. Determined to halt the march of the Crone once and for all, hatred becomes Heather's ultimate weapon and furies collide to devastating effect.

Crone – winner of a *Chill with a Book Readers' Award* (February 2018) and an *Indie B.R.A.G Medallion* (November 2017).

Praise for *Crone*

'A real page turner, hard to put down.'

'Stunningly atmospheric! Gothic & timeless set in the beautifully described Devon landscape …. Twists and turns, nothing predictable or disappointing.' – Amazon reviewer

'Atmospheric, enthralling story-telling, and engaging characters' – Amazon Reviewer

'Full of creepy, witchy goodness' – The Grim Reader

'Wycherley has a talent for storytelling and a penchant for the macabre' – Jaci Miller

Beyond the Veil

Upset the dead at your peril... Because the keepers of souls are not particularly forgiving.

Death is not the end. Although Detective Adam Chapple has always assumed it is.

When his ex-wife is killed, the boundaries between life and death, fantasy and reality, and truth and lies begin to dissolve. Adam's main suspect for the murder, insists that she's actually his star witness.

She claims she met the killer once before.

When she died.

As part of his investigation, Adam seeks out the help of self-proclaimed witch, Cassia Veysie who insists she can communicate with the dead. However, the situation rapidly deteriorates when a bungled séance rips open a gateway to a sinister world beyond the veil, and unquiet spirits are unleashed into the world.

Can Cassia and Adam find a way to shore up the breach in the veil and keep the demons at bay?

With time running out and a murderer on the loose, the nightmare is only just beginning ...

Praise for Beyond the Veil

'A 5-star winner from Queen of the Night Terrors' – Amazon reviewer.

'Really got my heart pounding' – Amazon reviewer.

'A nerve racking, nail-biting, spine tingling, sweat producing, thrilling storyline that keeps you on a razor's edge the entire tale' – ARC reviewer.

'Female Stephen King!' – Amazon reviewer.

Coming in 2020

The Municipality of Lost Souls by Jeannie Wycherley

Described as a cross between Daphne Du Maurier's *Jamaica Inn*, and TV's *The Walking Dead*, but with ghosts instead of zombies, *The Municipality of Lost Souls* tells the story of Amelia Fliss and her cousin Agatha Wick.

In the otherwise quiet municipality of Durscombe, the inhabitants of the small seaside town harbour a deadly secret.

Amelia Fliss, wife of a wealthy merchant, is the lone voice who speaks out against the deadly practice of the wrecking and plundering of ships on the rocks in Lyme bay, but no-one appears to be listening to her.

As evil and malcontent spread like cholera throughout the community, and the locals point fingers and vow to take vengeance against outsiders, the dead take it upon themselves to end a barbaric tradition the living seem to lack the will to stop.

Set in Devon in the UK during the 1860s, *The Municipality of Lost Souls* is a Victorian Gothic ghost story, with characters who will leave their mark on you forever.

If you have previously enjoyed *Crone* or *Beyond the Veil*, you really don't want to miss this novel.

Sign up for my newsletter or join my Facebook group today.

Printed in Great Britain
by Amazon